Captivated

NEW YORK TIMES BESTSELLING AUTHOR

MEGAN HART

INTERNATIONAL BESTSELLING AUTHOR

TIFFANY REISZ

COSMO RED-HOT READS
FROM HARLEQUIN

Recycling programs
for this product may
not exist in your area.

ISBN-13: 978-0-373-62247-4

Captivated

Copyright © 2014 by Harlequin Books S.A.

The publisher acknowledges the copyright holders of the individual works as follows:

Letting Go
Copyright © 2014 by Megan Hart

Seize the Night
Copyright © 2014 by Tiffany Reisz

For questions and comments about the quality of this book, please contact us at CustomerService@Harlequin.com.

Printed in U.S.A.

CONTENTS

LETTING GO   7
Megan Hart

SEIZE THE NIGHT   117
Tiffany Reisz

DEDICATION

Dedicated to Shannon Barr and Ann Leslie Tuttle,
who keep me on track no matter how many times my emails go missing!

ABOUT THE AUTHOR

Megan Hart is an award-winning and multipublished author of more than thirty novels, novellas and short stories. Her work has been published in almost every genre, including contemporary women's fiction, historical romance, romantic suspense and erotica. Megan lives in the deep, dark woods of Pennsylvania with her husband and children and is currently working on her next novel for Harlequin MIRA. You can contact Megan through her website at www.meganhart.com.

Also by Megan Hart

Cosmo Red-Hot Reads from Harlequin

Crossing the Line (ebook)
You can also find *Crossing the Line* in the trade edition of *Tangled Up*

Dear Reader,

Let go!

That's something the heroine of my new Cosmo Red-Hot Reads from Harlequin story has a lot of trouble doing. At least she thinks so. The truth is that Colleen is a woman made to let go, give in to passion, set herself free to explore…even if she's convinced she's not capable of it!

Jesse, on the other hand, believes Colleen is more than capable of letting go. After getting to know her over several months of her regular Thursday-night visits to the bar where he works, he's developed a heavy-duty crush on this enigmatic woman who orders the same drink every week but never drinks it. It's not until a snowy night and a slow dance that the sparks ignite between them.

It's not easy, of course, but Colleen and Jesse manage to discover a mutual passion for the exchange of power and control. The rocky road to a relationship is set against the backdrop of one of my new favorite places, the Fell's Point neighborhood in Baltimore!

I hope you enjoy reading about Colleen and Jesse. And if the story gives you a craving for some good old-fashioned greasy diner food, well…what can I say? Breakfast is my favorite meal!

Thanks for reading,

M

LETTING GO

by

Megan Hart

CHAPTER ONE

"The usual?" The Thursday night bartender grinned at Colleen. He'd already filled her glass three-quarters with amber liquid and pushed it across the polished wooden bar toward her. He added a separate glass of seltzer water with a twist of lime, just the way she liked it.

Jesse, she thought as she brushed the dampness from her shoulders where the snow had melted. That was his name. "Thanks, Jesse."

Jesse's eyes narrowed for a moment. He looked her over and, coming to some sort of conclusion, said, "How about an order of onion rings?"

"I… Yes. Sure." Colleen bit back her initial protest, imagining how good something greasy and fattening would taste. It was exactly what she needed right now, but wouldn't have thought of ordering until he suggested it. "That would be great."

"You got it." Jesse rapped the top of the bar with his knuckles in a staccato pattern, then turned to take another order.

He'd leave her alone. And alone was what Colleen wanted

to be. So a few minutes later when a man in a business suit slid onto the stool beside her, she just stared at him when he delivered his pickup line.

The man stared back, rakish grin fading. "I said—"

"I heard you," she interrupted. "But I already have a drink."

The businessman tugged at his tie. "So it's like that, huh?"

"It's not like anything," Colleen said quietly.

"Hey, I'm just trying to be nice."

Colleen half turned away. "So then be nice."

When he put his hand on her elbow, his fingers pinching just a little too hard, she shoved it away. The businessman looked surprised. Then pissed. He put both hands up and backed off, but not before muttering something that sounded suspiciously like "Crazy bitch."

"Is there a problem?" Jesse balanced a platter of onion rings on his palm before setting it in front of her. "Hey, buddy. You got a problem?"

"No. Not at all." The businessman took his drink and slid down to the other end of the bar where an attractive brunette and her prettier friend were laughing as they took a cell phone selfie.

Colleen pushed her whiskey glass to the side to make room for the food. The liquor sloshed, splashing her a little. She used a napkin to wipe her fingers and looked up to see Jesse staring at her.

"You okay?"

She nodded. "Yeah. Thanks."

Jesse didn't leave, though there were people waiting to be served. He studied her in silence for a few seconds longer than seemed necessary. "Can I get you anything else?"

"Nope." Colleen gave him a small smile as she lifted an onion ring toward him. "This should do it."

"Did he bother you?"

Surprised, she lowered the onion ring without biting it. "I can handle myself. It's okay."

At the sound of raucous laughter, Jesse looked down the bar. The businessman was now taking a picture with the two girls. Jesse looked back at Colleen with a frown. "I know you can. I've seen you. I just wanted to be sure."

"You've seen me, huh?" She sipped some seltzer and dipped a ring into the horseradish sauce, but didn't bite.

"You come in here every Thursday night," Jesse pointed out. "I'm not saying we get a bunch of jackasses in here or anything, but there are some nights it feels like I'm Pinocchio on Pleasure Island."

Colleen laughed. The giggle slipped out of her, unbidden and certainly unexpected. It turned the head of the businessman at the end of the bar, who glared at both of them before turning back to his new friends. Colleen didn't let it get under her skin. She'd dealt with much worse.

"Bonus points for that reference," she said to Jesse.

"Been watching a lot of Disney movies, what can I say?" Jesse shrugged, leaned on the bar and grinned. Over his shoulder, he said to John, the other bartender, "Can you take care of that guy over there? Yeah, the one giving me the death stare."

John nodded and moved to handle the other customer. Colleen bit into her onion ring and gave Jesse the side-eye. It didn't seem to bother him, and his widening grin didn't seem to bother her.

"You're too old for Disney movies," Colleen said.

"Never too old for Disney."

"Too young for *Pinocchio*, then. You're more the *Hercules* and *Aladdin* era, aren't you?"

"I have all the classics," Jesse said. "My kid loves them."

She couldn't conceal her surprise. Jesse had been working on Thursdays for at least six months, but this was the first time she'd heard him mention a child. Of course, there'd never been reason for her to ask him if he had kids. Or anything else about him, really. They'd never had more than the most casual conversations, which had never seemed rude until just now.

Jesse laughed at her expression. She blushed, the flush creeping up her throat and all over her face, impossible to hide. Rosy cheeks always gave away her emotions.

"I...I didn't know. I mean, I...I didn't think," she stammered.

Jesse pushed upward with his hands, straightened and knocked on the bar again, rat-a-tat tat like a drumbeat. "Her name's Laila, and she's eleven. She claims she's getting a little too old for Disney movies, but I've convinced her that her old man needs an excuse to keep watching them."

"You don't look old enough to have an eleven-year-old," Colleen said. He couldn't be more than what, twenty-three? Maybe twenty-four, tops. A decade younger than her, at least.

Jesse stepped out of the way so John could get to some of the bottles on the top shelf behind him. He gave John a nod to acknowledge that it was time for him to get back to work. Still, Jesse took the time to give Colleen another slow smile that she supposed melted the panties off lots of ladies. She countered with another dip of onion ring.

"I'll be forty," he told her.

"What? Wait. No way!" she called after him. Patrons' heads turned for the second time that night.

"Eventually, if I'm lucky!" Jesse said over his shoulder and started taking orders at the bar's far end.

Colleen shook her head and caught John's eye. "Guess he showed me."

John, who'd been working at The Fallen Angel for as long as Colleen had been coming there, and probably for almost as long as the bar had been open, rolled his eyes. "He's a smart-ass and he's twenty-eight. You need something, hon? Another drink?"

"Another seltzer when you get a chance." She wiped her mouth with a napkin and emptied her glass to wash away the burn of horseradish.

John took the glass and filled it, then nodded at the untouched whiskey. "Freshen that for you?"

"No, thanks."

"Just let me know if you need something, hon." With that, John moved off to attend to another customer.

There was a reason why Colleen came to this place every week instead of visiting different bars. Or simply staying home, which was really where she wanted to be. She came to The Fallen Angel because they knew her here. Nobody ever made her feel as though she had to "pay rent" by buying more than her single drink. And they left her alone, mostly.

Except for Jesse.

He wasn't a bother. The opposite, as a matter of fact. He was…*attentive* wasn't quite the word Colleen was thinking of, though he was. It was more than that. He was considerate. Accommodating. *Solicitous.* As with the onion rings, he seemed to know what she wanted before she'd thought of it. Unlike John, Jesse didn't bother to ask her if she wanted her whiskey refreshed, though he filled her glass of seltzer once more without waiting to be told. The attention was just enough, and not too much.

At the end of the night, right before she pulled out her wallet to pay her check, he brought her a small dessert cup of chocolate mousse topped with a swirl of heavy whipped cream.

"On the house," Jesse said before she could protest. "Eat it. Trust me, you'll like it."

It was the second time that night he'd made an assumption about what she'd like. It wasn't a question of whether she would like it. It was that he seemed so sure of what she wanted that it became difficult for Colleen herself to be sure. She pushed the mousse away with her fingertips the way she'd earlier pushed the glass of whiskey.

"No, thanks." She handed him a twenty. "Keep the change."

Jesse caught up to her at the doorway. He came around the bar and tugged her by the sleeve. She yanked her arm free of his grip, which wasn't tight or hurtful yet still forced her heart to thump-thump-thump and her throat to close.

"Sorry," Jesse said. Colleen didn't say a word. He let go of her immediately and took a step back. "I just wanted to say...I'm sorry. I thought you'd like the dessert. I mean, who doesn't like chocolate? Unless...you're not allergic are you? Shit. I'm sorry, Colleen. I didn't think about that."

She could've been out the door already, into the dark street and heading for home. She cast a wary glance around the bar, but it was getting late, and on a Thursday the crowd was thinner than it would be on the weekend. Nobody was paying attention to them. Even the businessman had long gone.

"I'm not allergic."

"Oh. Okay." He smiled, gaze holding hers. "You don't like chocolate?"

"I like chocolate a lot. Who doesn't?" Colleen drew in a small breath to keep her voice steady. "I just don't like it when someone thinks he knows better than I do about what I want."

It was the wrong thing to say, or maybe the right one, because at her words, Jesse's gaze shuttered at once. His mouth thinned. He took another step back.

So did she.

Then she pushed through the door and out into the cold winter night.

"Don't tell your mom. She'll kill me for letting you eat that for breakfast." Jesse pointed at the small cup of chocolate mousse he'd brought home from work last night. Hey, he'd paid for it. He wasn't going to toss it in the trash just because his friendly gesture had been thrown back in his face, as if he'd been some kind of dick instead of a guy trying to be nice.

Laila rolled her eyes. "Duh."

"Hey, kid, I thought we had an agreement. You don't tell your mom when I let you stay up too late or eat crap for breakfast, and you don't bring me any of that vegetarian business she tries to send over this way." Jesse scrubbed at his face, bleary-eyed. The coffee couldn't brew fast enough. Six-thirty in the morning was too damned early when he'd only gone to bed at four.

Laila kicked her feet against the rungs of her stool and licked chocolate from her spoon. "Mom says next year I can stay home by myself until it's time for school."

Jesse, who'd decided he couldn't wait for the rest of the pot to fill and had begun to pour coffee into his mug, looked up. The coffeemaker hissed and spit on the hot plate until he put the carafe back. "What? Are you kidding?"

"I'll be *twelve*, Dad." The weight of tween scorn should've burned him worse, but Laila added such a sweet smile that Jesse was only a tiny bit stung.

"Twelve's old enough to stay home alone?"

"Mom says if I prove to her I can get up on my own with

the alarm and not need her to wake me up, sure. I got up on my own today," Laila said proudly.

It would make his mornings a lot less groggy, that was for sure. But it would also mean a lot less time with his daughter. Jesse frowned. "So…she's going to stop dropping you off on the way to work?"

"Dad," Laila said, exasperated. "Pay attention! Yes, that's what I mean!"

"But not until next year."

"Yeah, when I'm in sixth grade." Laila finished the last of the mousse and dumped the container in the garbage, then rinsed the spoon before putting it in the dishwasher. That was a trick her mother had taught her, that was for sure.

"Let's worry about it when you're in the sixth grade, then, okay?" Jesse yawned and finished pouring his coffee.

He added sugar and cream from the fridge, peering inside with an internal sigh. Empty. He needed to get to the store in the worst way, something he could easily do after dropping Laila at school, if he could stay awake long enough.

"Can I watch *The Little Mermaid* again?"

Jesse put the cream back in the fridge and yawned again until his jaw popped. Plopping his kid in front of cartoons was definitely a no-no according to her mother, who didn't even have cable television or the internet at home. But it would buy him another hour of sleep and a shower before they had to leave for school.

"Dad?"

"Yeah. Sure. Go ahead." Too much planning to do on less than three hours of sleep. He could mainline this coffee and it still wouldn't wake him up enough.

He ended up snoozing on the couch while Laila watched the movie, waking only in time to get her out the door. No shower first, so he pulled a knit cap over the mess of his hair and headed out into the world looking like, as his kid said, a hobo.

The drive to school was both eternal and too short. It took forever because he was tired and wanted to get back home so he could slide back into bed and get a few hours' sleep before he had to get up again. But it was not long enough, because it was time with his daughter, who filled it with stories about school and her friends and her thoughts on life. Always entertaining, usually surprising.

"And that," she told him as she opened the car door, "is why me and her aren't friends anymore."

"She and I," Jesse corrected automatically. He hadn't really followed the story of Laila and her no-longer-best friend Maddy, but understood enough to realize that whatever had gone down had been the fifth-grade equivalent of World War III. "And listen, she's your friend. Can't you work it out?"

Laila gave him a heavy sigh and paused, the backpack he couldn't believe she was strong enough to carry still on her lap. "Dad, you don't get it. She took my favorite pen! And lied about it!"

It was the lie that had made the crime unforgivable. He could see that. Still... "People make mistakes, kiddo."

"If she lies about a pen, what else would she lie to me about?"

She was too smart for him, the best of both her parents multiplied by ten. "True. But that doesn't mean you can't forgive her."

"I can forgive her," Laila said darkly, her brow furrowed. "That doesn't mean she can still be my friend."

With that, she got out of the car. Ignoring the impatient moms in minivans behind him who barely stopped to let their kids roll out before they sped off to Pilates or hot yoga or whatever the hell they were in such a rush to get to, Jesse

watched her until she got through the school doors. Then
he gave each of the scowling minivan moms a cheery salute,
using all his fingers when he really wanted to use only one.

He still needed food. An egg sandwich and another tall
coffee tried to woo him into the local 7-Eleven, but he reminded himself of his credit card bill, due next week, and the
upcoming tuition bill for Laila, due sometime next month.
The rattle under his car's dashboard helped remind him, too,
that his baby had just over a hundred thousand miles on her,
and she had to last him another year or so before he could
think about replacing her.

It was going to get better, he reminded himself. Private
school for his kid was important to her future, and sacrificing
for her was worth it. At home, a few more hours of sleep and
a shower put some lightness into the day. So did the dogs in
the shelter where he volunteered. Playing with them never
failed to brighten his outlook. His time there finished, Jesse
headed back to his car, pausing to look at the gray sky. It
looked like snow. Smelled like it, too. He was looking forward to a good winter storm. Which meant he definitely
had to get something in his fridge.

He didn't usually shop at this market, but this place was
conveniently close to the Angel. Armed with his reusable
bags from the trunk, the list he kept updated on his phone
and the small accordion file of coupons he collected from
the bar's Sunday paper every week, Jesse grabbed a cart and
hit the aisles.

And there she was.

The woman from the bar. Colleen, last name unknown.
Today, as usual, her pale hair was pulled back at the base of
her neck in a sleek bun. She wore a tailored black wool coat
that came to her knees, a hint of crimson liner at the throat
and sleeves, and below it a pair of black-stockinged legs and

librarian pumps with a strap across the top of her foot that, no kidding, left his throat a little dry. She carried a paper cup of coffee in one hand and pushed her cart, one of the little ones, with the other.

She wasn't watching where she was going. It was easy enough for him to let his cart bump hers, gently enough not to even slop her coffee. It was easy, but stupid, Jesse thought at the last second as she turned, frowning. Now he'd pissed her off.

Again.

"Sorry," she said, though it was clear she knew it was his fault. "Oh. It's you."

"It's me. Jesse," he added.

"I know your name. You work at The Fallen Angel." She inched her cart, containing a carton of eggs and a loaf of rye bread, away from his.

"And you're Colleen."

"Yes." She could've pulled her cart away and stalked off down the aisle without looking at him again, but instead she cleared her throat. "So...you shop here?"

Jesse looked at his own cart, empty at the moment. "Nah. I just come in, push a cart around for exercise. Beats the gym fees."

It had been a gamble, just as bumping her cart had been, but this time she laughed. Her face lit up. A man could fall in love with a woman who laughed like that.

"That was a stupid question. Sorry." Colleen sipped her coffee, her large gray eyes meeting his over the rim of the cup without sliding away.

Those eyes. Shit. He was a goner.

For weeks he'd been getting to know her little by little. At first she was only another customer, but over time he'd begun to notice the things about her that stood out. The quiet way she sat by herself, never engaging anyone in more than the barest of conversations. Sometimes she read a book. Sometimes she toyed with her phone while she ate some pub food, usually onion rings but sometimes fries. Once or twice, she ordered a basket of fish and chips.

The glass of whiskey she ordered every week without fail, but never drank.

But although they'd had their share of casual interactions, had she ever looked at him until right now? Really looked, as if she actually saw him? She had, fleetingly, last night, and it was obvious she hadn't cared much for what she'd seen. Now she was looking at him again, her gray gaze pinning him, and he found himself struggling a little for words.

"My father used to say there are no stupid questions," she continued as though there hadn't been a minute of painfully awkward silence between them. "Just stupid people."

"I was being a jerk. Trying to be funny. I'm an idiot."

She laughed again, not as loud, but the sound was as lovely the second time as it had been the first. That laugh dug into him, between his ribs. Into the tender places beneath.

"I need to get going. I'll be late for work." She lifted her coffee cup his way in something like a salute. "See you…?"

"Next Thursday," Jesse said, and found himself wishing it were tomorrow instead of next week.

CHAPTER TWO

Colleen pressed her fingers deep into the sore spot just below her ear. An old injury flared up whenever she got tense, which had been happening a lot recently. Of late, circumstances had required her have more to do with Steve than usual. No matter how she tried to never let her ex-husband get under her skin, he was still an expert at it. Probably always would be.

As if Mondays weren't hard enough, this morning it had been a series of texts about repairs that needed to be done on the house they still shared in Rehoboth Beach, Delaware. When their marriage ended, she'd been desperate enough to walk away with next to nothing just to be rid of him. If she'd been able to afford to buy him out, she'd have done it. But the only other option had been letting the place go altogether, and she didn't want to give up the ocean. Not even to be entirely rid of Steve.

Still, although they'd kept the condo and shared responsibilities for it, somehow it had become Colleen's job to oversee them and Steve's to criticize. Not that she was surprised.

Despite Steve's constant protests to the contrary, it had been that way throughout their marriage.

She didn't have time for him today. Work was kicking her ass. It was her job to keep everything running smoothly and act as a liaison between the small mom-and-pop operation being consumed by the company she worked for, QuidPro-Quotient. Usually Colleen enjoyed working with smaller companies, helping them to make the transitions. Despite how ravenous QPQ had become over the past few years, Colleen believed in the company's mission statement.

Enfold, embrace and embark on new adventures.

There wasn't much embracing going on right now. Matt Lolly, the former owner and president of Lolly and Pop Computers, had agreed to sell his family business more than six months ago, but had not yet let go of the reins.

She thought about the conversation they'd had earlier that day since Mr. Lolly was...malingering. "I understand," Colleen murmured, keeping her voice and expression neutral. "But believe me, Mr. Lolly, you are going to be leaving your grandchildren a legacy. Perhaps not the actual shop itself, but with the money you'll be able to put aside for them..."

"I started that shop with my own dad, and then worked in it with my sons." Mr. Lolly gave her a fierce look. "Money can't replace any of that."

Since he'd sold the company because both his sons had gone to find other jobs, and none of the grandchildren seemed interested in taking it over, his rationale wasn't quite on point. But Colleen knew what he meant. She'd spent a lot of hours with her own dad in his workshop. Money could never buy back those hours.

"Mr. Lolly, I understand your reluctance."

He gave her a stern stare. "I don't think you really do. You're going to buy my shop and turn it into some kind of fast-food restaurant type of place. My customers expect a certain level of service—"

"Your customers," Colleen interjected, "are all buying their computers online or down at the Apple store, and taking them there to be fixed."

Silence.

Mr. Lolly cleared his throat. Colleen expected to feel bad about the way she'd snapped, but the fact was, she'd been working with this guy for months, and he was still fighting her every inch of the way. She understood his reasons. She'd done her share of not letting go of things that no longer served her. But she no longer cared.

"You've signed a contract," she told him. "You've been paid all but the final amount. Mr. Lolly, it's time you signed off on the rest of the agreement. Okay? I have a check right here for the final payment. You could go on a nice, long vacation. Or put this money into a retirement fund. Or send your grandkids to college. But if you don't sign, I'm going to have to declare this agreement void, and you'll have to pay us back what you've already accepted."

He looked startled at that. "But I've—"

"Sign off," she told him gently and handed him a pen. All QPQ needed was his final signature releasing QPQ to take over the daily operations, including the hiring and firing of the current employees.

"You said they'd keep their jobs," he said finally. "It's just the two of them."

"Or that they'd get a nice severance. And they will." Her company actually had no desire to keep Lolly and Pop Computers in business. She'd been instructed to buy out the company for its inventory and real estate, a prime location on the main street of a small town. What QPQ's owner decided to do with all of that, Colleen didn't know. Also didn't care.

Mr. Lolly sighed. Then sighed again. He hung his head, but if he thought puppy eyes were going to gain him any sympathy from her... Colleen put on a smile. She pushed the pen across the desk to him.

"Please sign, Mr. Lolly."

He did, but with a resentful look she took as an affront, even though she didn't react to it. At the doorway, the check still clutched in his hand, he turned to her. "It just seems like a very cold way to do business, that's all."

He didn't give her time to respond, and even if he had, what might she have said? Colleen wasn't the one who'd pursued the sale or even closed the deal. It was her job to see difficult acquisitions through to the end, that was all. And she was good at it. Over the years, she'd sold her soul to the devil for the ability to support herself.

With the plunging temperatures outside and bad weather in the forecast, all she really wanted to do tonight was put the day behind her, take a hot bath, get into a bed made up with fresh sheets and go to sleep. Her sleep last night had been interrupted again by bad dreams about losing her dad. About waking up in bed next to Steve, their divorce being the dream instead.

But it was Thursday, she reminded herself as she poured another cup of coffee from the office communal pot. Thursday meant The Fallen Angel and her ritual.

"Colleen." It was Mark, looking dapper as usual in a three-piece suit complete with pocket watch. "You took care of Lolly?"

She nodded. "Yes. He signed, took the check. I passed everything along to Jonas."

Jonas would take care of the final settlement with the Lolly and Pop Computers employees.

Mark grinned and poured himself a cup of coffee. Then he made a face.

"This is swill!"

Colleen laughed. "Um, well, yes. I tried to tell you not to buy the coffee service company. You didn't listen."

"I can be a fool." Mark pulled a sad face so exaggerated that she laughed again.

He narrowed his eyes, looking her over, up and down. "Turn around."

"No…"

"Colleen, turn around."

"I'm going to sue you for sexual harassment," she muttered, but did a slow twirl.

Mark huffed. "Go ahead. That skirt doesn't suit you at all. Why do you insist on covering up your legs? They're gorgeous. And those shoes, my God. A nun would think they're dowdy."

"I like these shoes." Colleen looked down at her outfit. She had a few pairs of heels she wore to the office, but today, with the bad weather alert, she'd gone with a serviceable pair of loafers paired with thick tights and a long wool skirt. "Anyway, this is warm."

"But it's *so* not hot." Mark shook his head. "I should fire you."

She looked up, startled, to see if he was joking. "You wouldn't!"

"I like pretty things. This makes me sad." He waved a hand at her ensemble with a serious look.

She wouldn't put it past him to fire her for her fashion faux pas. He was just unstable—and rich—enough not to care if there were repercussions. Colleen lifted her chin. "Too bad. I'm not here to look good. I'm here to do my job."

She paused. Both of them stared each other down.

"Besides," she added, "you act like I come in here every day looking frowsy. And that, I know for a fact, is not true."

Mark smiled and tipped his head back in laughter loud enough to make Jonas and Patty both peek over their cubicles to see what was going on. He spilled some coffee on the floor in his delight, which made him put his mug on the counter. He pointed at the coffee station.

"Get someone to take care of this. This is disgusting. And you," he said to Colleen, "leave early today. Get that abomination out of my office before it makes me puke."

"I have work to finish," she said mildly, but Mark cut her off with a furious hand gesture and a scowl.

"Out!" He said. "As a matter of fact, everyone, out! Go home early today. It's going to be wretched out later. And take tomorrow off, too. I don't want to see any of you until Monday."

"We'll still get paid, right?" Patty popped her head up again. She was already pulling on her coat.

"Maybe." Mark had turned, heading for his office.

Jonas coughed. "You have to, Mark. It's in our contracts. We get paid when you close the office."

"Fine, fine, fine." Mark didn't look over his shoulder, just disappeared into his office and closed the door.

Jonas, Patty and Colleen shared a look. Of the three of them, Colleen had known Mark the longest. Her relationship with him was the most complicated because of their history, but that didn't mean she liked him any better than anyone else did. Colleen was grateful to Mark. She always would be. But he wasn't easy to deal with on any level.

"He's such a pain in the ass," Jonas said, clearly agitated.

Mark's office door opened. "I heard that. I should fire you."

Jonas slowly, slowly, slowly raised his middle finger. Patty let out a muffled giggle. Mark slammed the door.

"He can't fire me, ever," Jonas said. "I added it to my contract, and he signed it, that crazy jackoff."

It was not the best of office environments, but then it was also never boring.

Back in her office, Colleen quickly checked her appointment calendar, made a few calls to rearrange some things due to the "weather-related office closing" and shut down her computer. Getting out of work unexpectedly early was the equivalent of a snow day in elementary school, and she intended to make the most of it.

She'd been to the market earlier in the week, but made another trip now to stock up on milk, bread, eggs, toilet paper and chocolate, the staples for any snow day. She added some tortilla chips and salsa, a few gossip magazines and, on impulse, a bottle of bath oil some clever stock person had featured near the romance novels and a display of funky battery-lit candles with lights that flickered. She bought some of those, too.

It was lucky Mark had let them go early, because by the time she'd finished her shopping, the store had been nearly emptied of the same kinds of things she was buying. Two women almost got in a fistfight over toilet paper. And outside, the first white, fluffy flakes had begun falling.

In the ten-minute drive back to her apartment, the snow had become thick enough to make it hard for her to see, even with the windshield wipers going nonstop. Colleen pulled into her parking spot, not looking forward to having to dig herself out and do the parking-space shuffle. Last year, two of her neighbors had nearly come to blows over a space. Life in the city, she thought, remembering the heated driveway and three-car garage she'd given up when she left Steve.

Even if she had to shovel herself out from under three feet of snow and defend her spot in hand-to-hand combat, it was worth it.

The snow had made darkness fall even earlier than usual for January, and by three-thirty Colleen had turned on all the lights in her living room. She'd started a Crock-Pot of chili simmering for tomorrow, with some baked mac 'n' cheese for tonight's dinner. Comfort food, perfect for winter weather. She'd put on some soft music and pulled out a book to read, wondering if it was too early to get in the bath. If she waited a while longer, she could go to sleep right after. She could watch a movie in bed. She could stay up late playing games on her phone. She could eat whatever she wanted, sleep however she wanted, wear whatever she wanted.

Do whatever she wanted.

And as always, even four years later, this freedom sent her spinning in dizzy, delightful circles in her living room until everything slipped sideways and she had to sit down, hard, to keep herself from falling.

Colleen clapped her hands to her face to hold back the laughing sobs that tore at her throat and made her stomach sick. Nothing came without a price, especially freedom. She could do what she wanted because she'd sacrificed a lot to have it.

It was still Thursday, but the weather outside made anything but an emergency too much to deal with. And it wasn't an emergency, was it? To sit at the bar and order that drink the way she did every week? Nothing bad would happen if she didn't do it. And maybe, Colleen told herself, it was time to stop going at all.

And then her phone rang.

CHAPTER THREE

"When I was a kid, you had to listen to the radio station at five in the morning to figure out if school was canceled." Jesse held his phone up to John's bored face. "Now they text you the night before. So, hey, at least I don't have to get up early."

John tossed a towel over one shoulder and leaned over the bar to look out the front windows as best he could. "We should close early. Nobody's gonna come out in this mess, and anyone who's here should be getting home, anyway. Hell, I want to get home. It's nasty out there."

All the storm watch warnings had been right on target for once. The flurries had started that afternoon and grew increasingly heavier as the day passed. The weather forecast was calling for six to eight inches of snow by 2:00 a.m., which was normally when Jesse was closing up and heading home. But John was right—the weather was bad enough that if they could shuffle out the three people gathered around the table in the front, it would make sense to close up early.

As it turned out, the trio was finishing their drinks and

signaling for the check even as John started running the register receipts and getting the few glasses that had come out of the kitchen back on the shelf. He told the small kitchen staff to pack up and head out, then turned to Jesse.

"Let's get out of here."

Just as Jesse was getting ready to agree, the bell over the door jingled, and in she came. Colleen, the Thursday night special with the sad eyes and love of onion rings. He'd been certain she wasn't coming tonight and telling himself that he didn't care. But here she was, stamping her feet and brushing the snow off the shoulders of her heavy black coat. White flakes covered her light blond hair. In the few seconds before they melted, they looked like a circlet of flowers.

"We're—" John started.

"I got her," Jesse said, already pouring the glass of whiskey, neat, and sliding it into the spot she always took.

"You'll close up?" John asked.

Jesse barely gave him a glance. "Yeah. I'll take care of it. Lock up the back, okay?"

"Got it." John clapped him on the shoulder, gave Colleen a nod as he passed, and then…

They were alone in the bar.

"Nice night." Jesse twisted a wedge of lime into the glass of seltzer and put that in front of her, too. He'd meant it as a joke, but Colleen gave him a blank stare. No smile.

"Yeah, it's great. Thanks." She pulled the glass of seltzer closer, but didn't take a drink. She looked at the whiskey, and her mouth twisted.

Something was wrong. She was always quiet, but polite, and though he'd seen her give more than one hopeful douche bag the cold shoulder, she'd always been nice to Jesse. Well, until last week, when he'd somehow pissed her off. He hadn't meant to, had felt terrible about it. She'd seemed okay to him in the market, though. It didn't seem like she was holding a grudge. No, something else had closed off her face like a mask.

She'd been crying.

It didn't take a genius to see the faint streaks of mascara smudged under those beautiful gray eyes or the shadows beneath them. Those sad eyes. He'd always been a sucker for the girls who cried.

"Can I get you something else?" he asked carefully, too aware of how last Thursday he'd pushed the onion rings and mousse on her, thinking he knew what she wanted when he obviously didn't. "The kitchen's closed, but I can do a few things back there. If you want."

"Closed?" She blinked slowly. Understanding dawned. She flinched, looking around. "Oh. Shit. Oh, yeah, you're closed? I didn't think about it, the weather. It's so bad. I'll just go. I'll go now."

But she didn't go. She sat motionless, frozen, one hand on the seltzer glass and the other on the edge of her stool, as though she needed to push herself off it to get moving. A rivulet of icy water trickled from the melting snow in her hair, down her temple and over her cheek like a tear.

She looked at him then, though it was clear she didn't really see him. She shook her head, that gorgeous hair falling over her shoulders and half covering her face. It was the first time he'd seen it worn down, and he wanted to fist his hands in it. Tip her head back. Find her mouth with his.

Jesse had known he had a crush on her, but this was getting out of hand.

"I should go," she said again. And then, incredibly, she did something she'd never done before in all the months he'd been working Thursday nights. She picked up the glass of whiskey, and she drank it. She wiped her mouth with slightly shaking fingers. "I should go."

"No," Jesse told her. "Stay."

Uptight, controlling bitch.

The words echoed in Colleen's head, over and over. Steve's words. She'd heard them a thousand times before and had convinced herself they no longer stung. That he could no longer control her, no longer hurt her. Somehow, that self-delusion had made it worse.

You can't make it without me, can't make a decision, can't take care of anything, without me. I have to do it all for you, Colleen. You need me.

You need me.

Colleen swallowed against the smoky flare of the whiskey. It had gone down a little rough, but now warmth spread through her. She looked at Jesse. "Stay?"

"What else are you going to do? Go out into the cold? Not just yet," he told her with that smile, that damn smile she'd been trying to ignore all these nights when she came in to prove a point to herself.

A point she'd failed to make tonight. Or maybe it was the opposite. Maybe tonight was the first time anything she'd done had made sense.

She didn't need Steve, and hadn't for a long time. She never would again. She wouldn't need anyone again, she thought, finally looking at Jesse. Really looking at him, that smile, that earnest look. No more need, she told herself.

But she could *want.*

Colleen let her tongue dent her lower lip, where the whiskey flavor still lingered. It was not her imagination, was it, that Jesse watched her do it? Or that something in his gaze flared? Embers that had been banked so long inside her she'd have sworn they'd gone cold kindled at the sight of his look.

"You don't have to get home?" she asked him, pausing. Thinking. "Your kid?"

"She's with her mother. School's canceled tomorrow. So's her mom's work. They're all set." He put both hands on the counter and leaned a little closer with a head tilt that made everything inside her tumble and twist. "Can I get you another drink?"

The one she'd had was already softening the edges of everything. How long had it been since she'd had liquor? "Four years. Eleven months."

"Hmm?"

She looked at him. "The last time I had a drink was the night I finally decided to leave my husband. He goaded me into it. Both the drink and the leaving."

"What about tonight?" Jesse asked quietly.

"That," she said, "was him, too."

Without a word, Jesse pulled out a squat glass and poured a shot of Jameson into it, then another into her empty glass. He lifted his.

After a moment, she did, too.

It went down smoother this time. And somehow sweeter. Colleen shivered, not from the alcohol's burn but at the way Jesse was looking at her.

"He used to tell me all the time that I needed to loosen up. Lighten up. That I didn't know how to have a good time. That because I liked things a certain…way…" She paused, swallowing, not sure why she was telling him this. Only that she needed to tell someone. "He said I was a pain in the ass to live with. No fun. I was a boring, nagging bitch who had to control everything, but that I was incapable of doing anything on my own. He made me feel constantly incompetent. Oh. And, according to him, I was frigid, too."

Jesse coughed lightly.

Colleen laughed. Low at first, then louder, letting her head fall back. The sound was harsh, very little humor in it. She closed her eyes for a second, memories unfurling like a ribbon inside her head, before she opened them to focus on Jesse.

"I'm not," she said. "I just didn't like fucking him."

It was Jesse's turn to laugh, the sound sweet as honey and just as thick. He leaned on the bar, hands shoulder-width apart. Fingers slightly spread. "He sounds like an asshole."

"He was." She licked her lips, watching again as his eyes followed the movement of her tongue. His gaze warmed her more than the booze had; Jesse looked at her as though he wanted to eat her up.

It had been a long time since a man had given her that stare. No, that wasn't true. It had been a long time since she'd paid attention to a man giving her that look and wanted to return it. Colleen let her fingertips trace a circle of damp left behind on the bar by her now empty glass. She glanced out the front plate-glass windows to the cobblestone street outside. A few people walked past, laughing and tossing snow at each other. Night had fallen, hard and dark and deep.

"It's still snowing," she murmured.

"Good thing we don't have any place to go, huh?"

"Why did you let me stay, Jesse?"

His smile faded for a moment, just long enough for him to blink. Then he leaned a little closer. "Because...I thought you needed to."

She remembered him giving her the chocolate mousse, and how it had rubbed her the wrong way. Yet he'd done so many things for her over the past few months since he'd started here at The Fallen Angel. He'd come to know her preferences so easily and had made it so easy for her to come back, week after week.

"I told you how I feel about people assuming they know what I need."

He nodded and turned to press a button on the small remote that controlled the pub's sound system. In seconds the slow, distinctive beat of "Cry to Me" filtered through the speakers. It had been one of her favorites for years, first as a cut on a vinyl album she'd found as a teenager scouring thrift stores and then later, as an adult, an iTunes track. How had he known?

Like the whiskey and onion rings and mousse and everything else, Colleen thought, he just had.

CHAPTER FOUR

Jesse moved before he could second-guess himself. He went around the bar, one hand out. He didn't ask her to dance. He waited for her to take his hand.

She waited long enough that he was certain she wasn't going to, but then her fingers eased into his and squeezed. Colleen slipped off the stool, a little unsteady but catching herself so that she didn't stumble. She was in his arms half a minute after that, the two of them pressed close on the splintery wooden floor that wasn't really meant for dancing. On one of The Fallen Angel's good nights, when the crowds of Fell's Point filled this bar cheek to cheek and hip to hip, there would have been no been room for them to do this, but now he spun her out slowly and back in again to dip her.

She laughed as he pulled her up, and damn, that smile, that gorgeous chuckle, made him understand why men had claimed they'd die for their lady loves. Everything about this woman made him want to make her happy. Keep her safe. When she allowed him to pull her in close again, he took a long, deep breath against the fall of her pale hair.

She shivered, tensing, but he kept his grip steady so she

didn't pull away. He'd have let her go, of course. He wasn't grabbing her. Wouldn't force himself on her. But in another second she relaxed against him, her face in the curve of his shoulder. And yes, oh, shit, yes, her hand cupping the back of his neck.

They danced.

Someone had been messing with the controls for the sound system, and when the song ended, there were two beats of silence before the same one started again. He waited for her to pull away from him, but she didn't. They moved to that old song as though it was the first time they'd ever heard it, and Jesse let himself get lost in the heat of her body. The scent of her. The smoothness of her cheek against his.

She murmured something under her breath as the song came to an end for the second time, but he couldn't catch what she said. He paused, not wanting to ruin the mood. "Hmm?"

Colleen pulled away enough to look into his eyes. "I do like chocolate mousse. I like it a lot."

"I know you do," he told her.

"I've never ordered it here."

"I just…guessed," Jesse said.

Colleen's eyes flashed bright for a moment before she shook her head and gave a small, embarrassed laugh. "I was such a bitch to you that day, Jesse. I'm sorry."

"Don't worry about it." He settled his hands on her hips, fingertips just brushing the swell of her butt. He wanted to slide them lower, but didn't dare. Not when this was going so well.

She linked her hands behind his neck. The song had started a third time, and both of them moved in a small circle. With every step, her body rubbed his. It was going to get embarrassing in a few minutes, but he didn't stop.

"Do you think I'm pretty, Jesse?"

He didn't hesitate for a second. "I think you're beautiful."

She laughed.

It seemed impossible that he could pull her closer, but somehow he managed. "What? You don't think so?"

"If enough people tell you that you're beautiful, you can easily start to believe it, right?" Colleen's mouth twisted wryly. "And yet it only takes one person to tell you that you're ugly to make anything anyone else ever said feel like a lie."

"Did he tell you that you were ugly?" The ex-husband, the asshole.

"No." She shook her head. "He never had to say it out loud. He just made me feel that way."

"He's—"

"An asshole," she cut in. "I know."

It was the perfect time to kiss her, so he did. He could tell himself he meant it as a sweet gesture, only friendly, but the moment his mouth pressed hers, it was all he could do not to crush her against him. And when her lips parted, opening for him, and her tongue slid along his, Jesse broke the kiss with a small, mortifying groan.

Colleen shuddered. The brightness had gone out of her gray eyes, replaced by something hazier. Heavy-lidded. She slipped her tongue along her lower lip the way she'd done a few times already tonight, each time sexier than the last. She hadn't moved away from him, and now his cock was definitely making itself known. She had to feel it against her. She had to.

The song ended and began again. She looked toward the bar. He didn't want to let her go long enough to change the song, but as he started to, she turned to him.

"Let's get out of here."

Jesse paused, an unwelcome but also relieving space between their bodies, his hands still on her hips. "Where do you want to go?"

"I live two blocks away." She let her hands slide down his arms to entwine his fingers with hers and squeezed them.

Everything inside him knotted and tangled. Jesse studied her, searching for signs that the whiskey had made her too drunk to be rational. It wouldn't have been the first time a woman invited him back to her place. Drunk twentysomethings on a pub crawl, tipsy cougars out to prove to their friends they still had what it took, bachelorette party beauties trying to be memorable and make memories. Colleen wasn't like any of them.

Maybe she was messing with him. Revenge for pissing her off? Playing a game?

She looked into his eyes. Shadows shifted there. Something dark, but definitely aware. She knew what she was doing and what she wanted, yet still he hesitated until she spoke again.

"Come home with me, Jesse." If it had been a question, his common sense might've taken over and let him decline, but she hadn't said it that way. No hesitation, no question. A command.

They'd run the last half block, laughing and grabbing up snow to toss at each other. No plows had passed, which would make the morning an infinite pain in the ass for anyone trying to get in or out of any of the narrow, cobblestoned Fell's Point streets. With the snow still coming down at an inch or so an hour, already more than the weather forecasters had predicted, they'd be lucky if they got shoveled out by Monday.

She was going to get lucky, Colleen thought as her key chattered in the lock because her numbed fingers couldn't quite fit it on the first try. With Jesse on her heels, she shoved open the front door, which stuck as usual because it was hung a little crooked. The pair of them stumbled into her dark foyer, lit only by the streetlamp outside. She slammed the door behind him, hard, to make sure it closed all the way.

"Don't worry," he told her. "I'm not going to try to escape."

Colleen hung her keys on the small hook beside the door and loosened her coat. Tossed it onto the newel post. She was so cold her teeth chattered worse than the key, and she'd lost feeling in her toes, but when she stepped up to pull him by the front of his shirt, all she felt was heat. "Kiss me."

He did. Softly at first, but harder when her mouth opened. His hands dug into her hair, fingers scraping her scalp like the best sort of deep massage, and it was her turn to moan. With her fingers still twisted tight in the front of his coat, Colleen stepped back, back, back until she hit the wall next to the arched doorway to the living room.

His hands were all over her. His cock, deliciously hard through his jeans, pressed her in just the right spot as he shifted, and Colleen gasped. Jesse's mouth moved from hers to nibble at her chin, and then yes, oh, God, yes, her throat. His teeth scraped her, sending arousal in red pulsing waves all through her.

"Touch me, Jesse." The words slipped out of her. Too much. Too harsh? But instead of sneering or laughing at her, Jesse groaned. One hand moved between her legs, his knuckles rubbing her clit through the sleek fabric of her winter-weight leggings.

Somehow they were moving again, this time into the living room, where she fell back onto her plush sofa with him on top of her. He moved, crotch grinding against hers. His kisses were fire, burning her up. But he was a little big, a little too heavy. Overwhelming. Without thinking, she pushed and rolled, ending up straddling him with her thighs pressed to his.

Colleen, breathing hard, sat up, one hand pressed flat on his chest. The other went to his belt buckle. She wanted to get him naked and have her way with him. She wanted to climb up his body and get his mouth on her clit, to ride his face until she came.

Yet she faltered. Her fingers had worked open his belt but not the button or zipper, and she paused. Her heart pounded. The whiskey had warmed her, loosened her, but she was far from drunk.

What the hell was she doing?

In this dim light, it would've been impossible to see the color of his eyes, but she knew they were a bright, pale blue. A striking combination with his near-black hair. Jesse was a handsome guy. More than handsome. Gorgeous. She'd seen the way the women who went to The Fallen Angel flirted with him, and how he'd always been pleasant but professional. Yet here he was with her. Why?

His eyes had been closed, but now he opened them and sat up a little bit. "Colleen? Are you okay?"

She'd asked him here. No. She'd *told* him to come with her. She'd practically attacked him in the front entryway. And now she was on top of him, tearing off his clothes. Colleen swallowed against a suddenly bitter taste.

"I…I'm sorry," she managed to say. "I'm not usually this… demanding."

Jesse's hands rubbed her thighs, moving up to settle on her hips and keep her in place when she tried to get off him. "Don't be sorry."

Controlling bitch, echoed Steve's voice. She tried to push it away, but the memories rose up again. Bitter. Hateful. His mockery, disdain, contempt and, finally, derision. *Always have to have it your way, huh? Can't just take it like a woman should? Frigid, boring bitch. Maybe get a few drinks in you, maybe that'll make you more fuckable.*

Colleen shook her head, scattering her ex-husband's taunts. She drew in a breath, looking down at Jesse. At least the dim lighting made this a little less embarrassing. Gave her a little extra courage. She got off him, anxious for a second when it seemed like he wouldn't release her. She sat next to him on the couch, close but not quite touching.

Jesse turned toward her. "Hey. You okay? Look, we don't have to...um... I don't want you to think we have to. If you don't want to."

"I want to." That was the truth, though she said it in a low voice, half hoping he wouldn't hear. "It's just that it's been a while. And I'm not sure I can. Come, I mean. I'm not sure."

Silence. She counted the beat of her heart. Five, then six thumps before he spoke.

"I'd like to help you, if I can." Jesse cleared his throat lightly. "Shit, that sounded cheesy. I mean I'd like to... Shit, Colleen, I want you. Have for...well, long enough. I'd like to make love to you."

That made her laugh, too loud. "You mean fuck."

"I'd like to fuck you, yeah." Jesse's voice was closer to her ear than she'd expected. His breath, warm on her face. He didn't touch her, though. "I'd like to make you come. I'd really like that."

Her need had made her greedy, but when she kissed him, it was slower and softer than it had been. Less frantic. When he moved closer to put his arms around her, she let him. It went on that way for a while. The kissing deepened. His hands moved over her, gently at first, a little harder if she moaned or sighed. Their clothes came off, and being naked with him was less nerve-racking than she'd have imagined, if only because the room was still so dark.

When his hand moved between her legs, stroking, Colleen shivered and twitched. Her breath caught. When he pushed her back against the cushions, murmuring a question about condoms, she blinked.

"I don't have anything." How stupid had she been? Inviting him back here with no preparation.

"Hold on." He pushed off her, but he was back in half a minute. "I have one in my wallet."

Flashbacks to high school made her sit up. Without his heat, she was starting to get cold. "Is that a safe way to keep it?"

"I have a special wallet," Jesse told her. He was silent for another second, then sounded half embarrassed. "It's got a special pocket."

"Oh." At this she sat up and pulled her knees to her chest. "You must use a lot of condoms."

She heard the hesitation in his answer, but then he moved closer to brush his lips over hers as he replied, "I believe in always being prepared. That's all."

Then he was moving over her again. Hands, mouth, teeth. His fingers slipped between her legs, making her shiver and shake, but then moved away. She waited, tense, for him to push her legs apart. To enter her. She wasn't going to come, not even close to it.

"Let go," he whispered. "Let me make you feel good, Colleen."

But she couldn't, that was the trouble. Steve had been right, she was too controlling. Too uptight. A sobbing breath hitched out of her. This was going wrong. She wanted it to be over so Jesse would leave. She stroked his fully erect cock, concentrating, listening to the sound of his breathing get faster. She sheathed him and positioned herself, ready.

But instead of pushing inside her, Jesse shifted on the couch so he could be on his back. She'd bought this sofa, love at first sight, because of how wide it was. Plenty of room for him to stretch out, no cushions in the way. He tugged her along with him, urging her to straddle his thighs the way she had before. His cock jutted between them. His hands pressed her hips for a second, his thighs bunching beneath them. When she touched him, his cock jumped. Jesse moaned softly.

He put his arms over his head, his fingers linked.

Everything inside her blazed. Her breathe soughed out of her, hitching in her throat as she did her best but failed to hold back a moan of her own. The muscles in her belly tightened. Her pussy clenched.

Colleen let her fingers drift over his belly, feeling his muscles leap and twitch. She looked at his face, his closed eyes. His tightened lips. Jesse's hips pushed upward.

Slowly, slowly, Colleen seated herself on his cock. Her thighs gripped his hips. She waited for him to move, to grab her or to start thrusting. To take control.

But Jesse didn't. He acquiesced to her every move with his own soft sigh and the shudder of his body. He throbbed inside her.

She didn't move.

Not for some long minutes as she concentrated on the feeling of him filling her. The beat and pulse of him inside her. He strained, shivering, but didn't move more than with the subtle shift of his in-and-out breath.

His hands stayed locked over his head. And that, oh, that giving up, that giving *in*… Her hips rolled, finally, unable to stay still. She wanted—no, needed—to move on him. To feel his thickness sliding in and out of her.

"You feel so good," he whispered.

More heat flooded her, rising up her throat to paint her face. She rocked on him, her clit rubbing his belly every time she moved. He would grab her now, she thought. Change up the rhythm to suit himself. And then it would be a rush to see if she could finish getting off before he did. But Jesse didn't do that. His eyes opened, locking with hers. He thrust, but in time with her motions. His fingers unlinked.

"No," she said suddenly. Harder than she meant to. "Keep them like that."

She thought he'd protest, or sneer, or, worst of all, laugh, but instead his gaze went dreamy and heavy-lidded. His hands locked tight to each other again. And best of all, he groaned, his throat working with that sound of pleasure as he arched and moved beneath her.

"How good do I feel?" Her voice didn't sound like her own.

"So good."

She rode him harder, desire rising. Her fingers dug into his lean sides, and Jesse gasped. "Tell me how good."

"So fucking good." His voice broke, rough and rasping. "Fuck, Colleen. You feel like heaven."

She slipped a hand between them to stroke her clit while she fucked him. Her pleasure spiraled higher and higher, everything coiling and twisting and tangling as she rocked on his erection. She was lost in the ecstasy, urged on by the look in his eyes and the grim press of his lips. The sweat on his forehead. He groaned again, and she almost came from the sound of his pleasure.

They moved together, faster, in perfect time. Her climax teased her, just out of reach. She wasn't going to make it, and anxiety pierced her again, making her want to move more desperately—if only to get him off so she could pretend she had.

And then she looked again at his linked fingers. The bulge of his muscles in his arms and the tendons of his wrists showed his struggle to keep his hands together. And why? Because she'd told him to.

Then she was coming, no holding it back, and the rush and push of her orgasm stole her breath. She wept with it, though she didn't want to. She dug her nails into him, and Jesse bucked beneath her. They finished together, and Colleen let herself fall forward to rest on his chest, her face buried against the side of his neck. They stayed that way, breathing hard, until his arms went around her, holding her close. And even though she hadn't told him it was okay, Colleen discovered it was the perfect thing for him to do.

CHAPTER FIVE

"I've never eaten here." Jesse pointed with his chin toward the front door of the Blue Moon Cafe, one of Fell's Point's most popular breakfast spots. "The lines are insane."

Colleen, that glorious hair tucked under a ridiculous knit cap, grinned and kicked the snow off her boots against the concrete steps. "Tourist."

"Hey!" he protested as he followed her into the tiny restaurant, furnished with an eclectic array of mismatched tables and chairs. "Unfair."

She laughed at him over her shoulder and waved at the waitress behind the counter. "Hey, Sheila. Wasn't sure you'd be open. But I had a craving for the French toast that just wouldn't quit."

"Mike made it in, so I did, too. But you might be the only customers." Sheila waved at the empty tables. "Take your pick. Might be the only time you ever see it this empty."

"There will be others," Colleen said. "Bad weather doesn't mean people won't need to eat."

The snow had fallen all night and halfway into the morning, tapering off but starting up again as they'd ventured out. They'd get another few inches, Jesse figured, not caring about being stranded because…damn. If you had to get snowed in, what better way to spend the weekend than with a sexy moon-haired goddess?

And she was a goddess, he thought, watching her surreptitiously as she looked over the menu. Last night had been incredible. Amazing. Thinking of it now, his dick tried to stir. There'd been a few moments when he'd been unsure that she really wanted him, or that she was enjoying it, but then wow. Something had triggered in her, and the way she'd taken charge had been incredible.

It had made him want to do anything to please her.

They both ordered the house specialty, Cap'n Crunch French toast, along with bacon and hash browns and coffee that Sheila brought in heavy-duty white mugs before going to the front door to look out at the snow.

"It's just not stopping," she said. "If I didn't live close enough to walk, I'd never have made it in."

"We'll get out of here as soon as we finish," Colleen told her. "Let you get home."

Sheila laughed and looked at Jesse. "Take your time. Hey, aren't you the bartender over at The Fallen Angel?"

"Yep." Jesse lifted his mug.

"Think you'll open later, when I want to get a drink? Kidding," Sheila said at the look on his face. "Totally kidding!"

Colleen leaned close to him when Sheila went into the kitchen. "She wasn't kidding."

"I wasn't scheduled to work this weekend anyway," he told her. He wanted to kiss her. He would have, if he thought she wanted it, but despite last night, this morning Colleen had been a little distant. Friendly. Flirtier, sure, than she'd ever been on a Thursday night. But not the way she'd been the night before.

"Do you think you'll try to get home?" She spun her mug around and around, not looking at him.

It wasn't what he'd expected her to say. It sure as hell wasn't what he wanted her to say. Before he could answer, Colleen spoke again.

"I don't even know where you live. You probably can't get home, huh? Certainly not if you have to drive. You should just…stay. With me." She looked at him then, her gray eyes faintly shadowed. "I mean, if you want to."

"If you want me to," he started, but went quiet when Sheila brought out their food. He waited until she'd settled everything for them before he said in a low voice, "I don't want you to feel like you have to invite me."

"Where else would you go?"

"I could crash at the Angel," Jesse said. "There's a bunk in the back room."

She stared at him for a heartbeat.

"I can't just leave you stranded." Colleen cut her French toast into precise squares and gave a nod, as though she'd made a decision and there was no changing her mind.

Not that he wanted to. But he didn't want to be a pain in the ass, either. "Look, really, I can hole up in the Angel if I have to. I don't want you to feel obligated just because we… because of last night."

She frowned. "Do *you* feel obligated because of last night?"

It wasn't the word he'd have chosen. *Hopeful* would've been a better choice. But he didn't want her to think he was just another horny asshole taking advantage of the situation, though. So all he said was, "Of course not."

Then the check came, along with Sheila's unspoken urging for them to finish their food and get the hell out of there so she and Mike could get home. Jesse grabbed it before Colleen could, holding it out of the way when she protested. He laughed when she tried to grab it, but she didn't.

"My treat," he told her. "For keeping me warm."

It came out wrong, he saw that at once when her frown deepened. She sat back in her chair. Her chin lifted.

They finished their meal in near silence after that. On the street, the snow was up to the bumpers of parked cars. The footprints they'd made on their way here had disappeared, not even a dimple in the white fluffy expanse to show anyone had been there at all.

"It's so quiet." Colleen's breath blew out in front of her in frosty plumes, and she gave him a sideways look. "And beautiful."

She was beautiful. And melancholy. The deadliest combination, as far as Jesse was concerned. It made him want to take care of her, which was going to be trouble, he knew it. He'd been burned before, such a sucker for the damsel in distress. He also knew it didn't matter. He'd get burned again.

Back in her town house, one of the really nice refurbished ones, he admired the gas fireplace in the living room. He hadn't noticed it the night before. Hell, he hadn't noticed anything but her.

"It doesn't work," she told him. "I mean, it probably works, but I haven't figured out how to do it."

He looked it over. "It's probably just the pilot light. I can start it for you. It might be nice to have a fire, huh?"

"Oh, I don't need—"

But he was already kneeling in front of the glass to twist the knobs and check the pilot light and the valve for the gas supply, both of which had indeed been turned off. It only took a few seconds of fiddling to get them both working and then turn on the fireplace. He grinned over his shoulder at her.

"Nice."

"It hasn't worked since I moved in. Thanks," Colleen said. "I didn't really need—"

His phone rang then, and he made an apologetic gesture before pulling it from his pocket. "Hey, kiddo. What's going on?"

"We're snowed in," Laila said. "Mom says it will be Monday before we can go anywhere. I'm bored! Can't you come get me?"

"I'm snowed in, too." Jesse sat back from the warmth of the fire, watching as Colleen bustled around turning on a ceiling fan and then rearranging the couch cushions they'd scattered last night. "Couldn't get you if I tried. You'll have fun with Mom. Don't worry."

"Where are you?"

"I'm at a friend's house." Jesse gave Colleen a glance, but she wasn't looking at him. "I'm okay."

"Daaaaad!" Laila sighed, ever the drama queen.

"Sorry, kid. Blame Mother Nature. Put your mom on the phone." He chatted with Diane for a minute or so, making sure they were both fine and laying out the child care arrangements for the next week. When he disconnected and set his phone on the coffee table, Colleen had just returned from the kitchen with a tray of mugs and a teapot.

"Everything okay?" she asked.

"Yep. Laila, that's my daughter. She's snowed in with her mom but was bored and wanted me to come get her. Her mom doesn't have cable TV." Jesse looked at the tray. "Coffee?"

"Cocoa. Is that okay?"

"Perfect." He moved to the couch, hoping she'd join him, but Colleen sat in the armchair across from him.

"How long were you married?"

"Oh." He paused. "We never got married. We had Laila when we were seventeen. We met at a party, got a little drunk. Did something stupid. We stayed together for a couple years and tried to make it work, but it was mostly over by the time we graduated from high school."

Colleen coughed lightly. "Oh."

"She lives with her mom most of the time, but we raise her together." Jesse poured cocoa for each of them and added marshmallows from the small bowl on the tray. "She's a great kid."

"I'm sure she is. We never had children. My ex, Steve, wanted a son. But we never got pregnant." She hesitated, then cleared her throat. "It's a good thing, really. If I'd had a child with him, I'd never have been able to leave him."

He wasn't going to argue with her about that, though he knew plenty of people who hadn't stayed together for the sake of the kids. "You've been divorced for...?"

"Officially, three years." Colleen took her mug, warming her hands but not drinking. When she put the mug back on the tray and fixed him with a look, Jesse braced himself. He'd seen that sort of look before. "I just want you to know something. Last night... I'm not usually like that."

"Hey, no judgment." Jesse shook his head. "We're both grown-ups. It seemed right at the time. It doesn't mean I think less of you or anything. And, believe it or not, I'm not usually one to just hop into bed with any random stranger, either."

"But when you do, you make sure you're prepared."

"Learned my lesson the hard way," he told her lightly. "I love my kid more than anything in the world, but it sure did make me a helluva lot more careful about sex."

"It's not the sex. Well, yes, the sex," she amended. "But not the fact we did it. Just...how it was."

He smiled at her. "You mean fantastic?"

Color rose in her cheeks, and her eyes glittered. "I mean how I was. With you. Telling you what to do and… Well, I'm not really that controlling, I'm really not like that. I don't have to have it all my way."

Her voice cracked. She picked up her mug and sipped, grimacing. She must've burned her tongue. The cocoa spilled over her fingers, and she yelped. Jesse grabbed up a paper napkin and pressed it to her hand, blotting the spill and taking the mug from her at the same time with his other hand. He set it down.

"You okay?"

"I'm fine!" She was clearly anything but fine as she got up to pace in front of the fireplace. "I just wanted you to know that I'm not like that. That's all."

"Like what? Powerful? Strong? Sexy as hell?" Jesse watched her without getting up.

She whirled to look at him. "Uptight and controlling and demanding and…needy! You think I needed you to fix my fireplace? That I couldn't do it on my own?"

"You didn't do it on your own," he pointed out.

"That doesn't mean I couldn't!"

Jesse bit back his defensive response, which left nothing but silence between them. She was breathing hard, her color high. Snow from earlier had melted in her hair, making it gleam. Like starlight. And damn him, he still wanted to bury his face in it and let her do whatever she wanted with him.

"I didn't think you were uptight or too controlling," he told her finally. "If you want to know the truth, I liked it when you took charge."

For a moment longer, she said nothing. Then she scoffed, "Sure you did."

"Colleen, do you really think I didn't have a good time

last night?" Jesse got up to approach her, but she took a step back and he stopped. "It was amazing, being with you. When you told me to keep still. The way you moved. I don't have to tell you how sexy you are."

"I'm not begging for a compliment, Jesse."

"It's not a compliment. It's an opinion."

Colleen's eyes narrowed, and she bit her lower lip. "You liked being bossed around?"

"Well. I can't say I love being bossed around in regular life, no. But in the bedroom, yeah. A little bit." He took a deep breath, thinking about it. "Okay, a lot."

"I'm not a dominatrix," she said flatly. "If you're expecting me to pull out the whips and chains and leather, you're going to be disappointed."

The idea of that, no lie, did get his cock a little thick, but he kept his expression neutral. "I'm not disappointed."

Colleen put her hands on her hips. "I just didn't want you to think that's how I am."

"But that *is* how you are," Jesse said.

"You think I like telling you what to do?" Her eyes blazed, but she didn't look angry. Not quite.

"Yeah." He took a step closer, waiting for her to pull away. She didn't. "I think you do. I think you get off on it, the way I get off on you doing it."

"Bullshit."

"What's bullshit is you trying to act like being in charge sexually makes you a controlling bitch, when one has nothing to do with the other." Jesse took another step toward her. Close enough now to grab her, though he made no move to do so.

"My ex said—"

"Maybe," Jesse told her, "you should think about letting

go of what your asshole ex-husband said and just do what makes you feel good."

She stifled a gasp. "You think fucking you made me feel good?"

"I know it did. And I'd like to do it again. And again, until you come so hard you can't stand up."

He'd blown it. Gone too far. He could see it in her eyes and the twist of her mouth and the way her shoulders squared. But Colleen surprised him.

"Take off your clothes," she said. "Now."

His hand went to his belt at once. Unbuckled. Unbuttoned. Unzipped. He shoved his jeans down his hips, past his thighs, and stepped out of them. She glanced at them when he kicked them away, but only for a second or so before her gaze fixed on his face. Jesse held Colleen's stare with his as he pulled his shirt over his head and tossed that, too. Standing in only his socks and boxer briefs, his cock already straining the soft fabric, he hooked his thumbs in the waistband and waited. Heart pounding.

"Everything," she told him. "I want you naked."

"Yes, ma'am." He'd tried to sound light, but failed. His voice was as thick with need as his hardening dick.

Colleen groaned softly, drawing out her reply, spoken so softly he barely heard it. "Ffffffffuck."

Naked in front of her, cock bobbing, he should've felt ridiculous. But when she circled him, admiring, letting one hand reach to trail along his shoulder blades and then down the line of his spine, all he could do was close his eyes and enjoy the caress. When she slid a hand to cup his balls, then stroke him, his knees buckled.

"Get on your knees," Colleen whispered. There was nothing of whips or chains in that command, nothing harsh. She said it as though she expected his worship, but did not yet believe she deserved it.

He didn't so much get on his knees as much as he melted onto them. His hands went naturally behind his back, wrists crossed at the base of his spine. He didn't think about why. She hadn't asked him for that. It just seemed right.

At the soft touch of her hand on his hair, he shuddered. Gooseflesh broke out all over him, though he was anything but chilled. Her hand passed over his head and then cupped his chin. She tilted his face to look up at her.

"You can go," she told him. "I can't make you stay. Or do this."

In reply, he turned his face to kiss her palm. He spoke against her skin. "Tell me what you want, Colleen. And I'll do it."

"I don't know what to ask." Her voice rasped. "I'm not sure how."

He leaned to press his face to her belly. She wore leggings. When he pushed his mouth between her legs he could feel the heat of her through them. He breathed out, adding the heat of his breath. Then the pressure of his mouth and chin.

"Do you want me to kiss you," he murmured, "here?"

"Yes. God, yes."

"Then tell me what you want."

"I want you to undress me," she said in a syrupy, dreamy voice. "Take off my clothes and eat my pussy until I come."

He was already tugging down her leggings to get at her bare skin beneath. The lacy scrap of her panties tickled his lips when he kissed her there. The smell of her filled his senses, making his head whirl. She moved, and he moved, turning so that she ended up sitting on the chair next to him. Still on his knees, he moved between her legs and covered her mound with his mouth. Breathing, sucking gently through the lace. He wanted his mouth on her bare skin so bad it hurt, but he was waiting.

"Panties off," Colleen said. "I want your mouth on me."

At the first taste of her, his cock throbbed. His balls ached. His hands slid up her thighs to open her to his questing tongue, then his fingers. He found her clit and flicked his tongue along it, then the seam of her, dipping briefly inside to taste her honey before finding her sweet spot again. He pushed a finger inside her, then another, moving them in time to the stroking of his tongue.

She tasted like heaven, but the sounds she made when he licked and sucked her were making him lose his mind. Right then there was nothing Jesse wanted more than to make this woman explode. He eased off, teasing her a little.

"Don't stop." Her hands dug into his hair, pulling him closer. Her hips rolled, pushing that sweet pussy against his mouth.

It was all he could do to keep up with her now. Jesse lost himself in making Colleen climax, teasing her swollen folds and the tight, hard knot of her clit until she cried out his name. Shit, he almost came just from the flood of sweetness she released on his tongue and the grip of her inner walls on his stroking fingers.

She shook, pulling his hair hard enough to make him groan. Then she eased off, relaxing back into the chair. Going limp.

"Oh, my God," Colleen said. "Do you think you could do that again?"

CHAPTER SIX

The best part of making mistakes was learning from them. Colleen's dad had said that often, always when she'd blundered in some way or another, although he'd always been good about never making her feel like an idiot for messing up. He would've said it about her marriage to Steve, she knew that much, if he'd been alive to see it happen. There were times when she'd wished the heart attack that had taken her father too young had spared him long enough to have said it. Other times, she was glad he'd never had to see her mess up so terribly in something so important.

What would he have said about Jesse?

She simply didn't know. It hadn't felt like a mistake at the time. Taking him home, spending the weekend with him. Fucking him until they were both weak-kneed and faint and aching in places she didn't know she had muscles. But on Monday morning, when he'd insisted on shoveling out her car for her before heading back to his own, it had begun to feel like she'd screwed up. Big-time.

He'd kissed her on her front porch, and she'd let him because it would've been impossible to refuse after the weekend they'd shared. Not unless she wanted to come across as, well, cold and frigid. Or rude. So she'd let him kiss her, even though it had felt too much like a promise she knew she couldn't keep.

He was too young. Too handsome. Too eager to please her. He made her feel too much in too short a time. She was ripe to be swept off her feet, seeing as how it had been a damn long time since she'd so much as kissed a man, much less had wild, passionate, unfettered sex with one.

This could only lead to misery and heartbreak. Hers. She felt the stirrings of it already, that yearning to see him again though it had only been a day since that last kiss. The constant checking of her phone to look for a text that couldn't possibly be there, since she hadn't given him her number. Yet still hoping he'd magically found it. Worse, the urge to saunter on down to The Fallen Angel all casual-like, even though it was not a Thursday and he might not be working. Or he might be, which wouldn't be any better, because then he'd know for sure she was there to see him, and he would know that she liked him. All of this was a giant platter of nope with a side order of hell no.

If Jesse had been a mistake, Colleen thought as she settled into work and tried without luck to stop thinking about him, what had she learned? That was the question. The problem was, she didn't know the answer.

When Colleen didn't show at The Fallen Angel for the second Thursday in a row, Jesse knew for sure it was because of him. She hadn't missed a week in the six months he'd been working there, and suddenly, after spending the weekend with him, she vanished? Definitely his fault. Which, shit, made him feel worse about being the reason for her giving up what had obviously been an important habit than he did about the fact she was doing it to avoid him.

The trouble was he honestly couldn't tell if she were giving him the brush-off because other than those Thursday nights and that one random time in the grocery store, he'd never had any contact with her. So on Monday morning, when the plows finally came and she'd looked out the window with a neutral expression and told him it was probably time for him to get home, all he'd been able to do was go. He hadn't asked for her number, something he was regretting now on Tuesday, because it had been a hella long day thinking about the next time he'd see her and having no idea if he would.

The weekend had been amazing. Not just the sex, though that had blown his mind. Just hanging out with her, watching old movies and playing cards had been incredible, too. He knew it was because of the snow, that they'd never have spent the weekend together that way so soon if they hadn't been snowed in. But that didn't stop it from feeling really, really right.

"John, I need to get out early." Jesse tossed his bar towel into the bin and started punching out of his shift without waiting for John's reply. He paused to stare at the other man when no answer came.

"Something wrong?" John asked at last, both eyebrows raised. "You sick? Tell me you didn't eat those nachos that were in the fridge, I know Rick said it was okay to eat what we found in the fridge, but those've been in there since September."

Jesse frowned. "No. And why doesn't anyone throw that shit away?"

"Why doesn't anyone do anything?" John gave him a blank look. "So where's the fire?"

Jesse finished clocking out and shrugged. "Got some things

to take care of. Anyway, you owe me, man. I stayed late the night of the snow."

"Whatever." John waved a hand and turned to a new customer asking for a draft. "It's your paycheck."

Jesse didn't care about that. He'd be able to pick up more hours next week if he wanted, because Rick hadn't yet hired anyone to take over during the day after that girl with the spiked hair, whose name Jesse had never been able to remember, quit. Sure, he'd be exhausted after working until three and getting up with Laila, but it was okay. He had something he had to do.

It might not be worth it, but he had to try.

Armed with a six-pack of hard cider, Jesse trudged through the still snowy sidewalks to Colleen's street. He hadn't paid attention to the house number, but Colleen's town house was easy to pick out because it was the nicest in the row. On the small concrete front porch, he raised a hand to ring the bell. Then stopped himself.

Shit, it was nine o'clock on a Thursday night, and she hadn't come into the bar for a reason. She was going to think he was some kind of crazy stalker for showing up here. And he was, kind of. Wasn't he?

Just before he could convince himself to turn around and walk away, her front door opened. Startled, Colleen let out a small shout and took two steps back. Jesse did, too, grabbing himself at the last second to keep himself from falling down the steps.

"What the hell?" she cried, a hand over her heart. She wore a pair of comfy-looking pajamas, the thin material showcasing her magnificent and clearly unconstrained breasts.

Jesse forced his eyes to meet hers as fast as he could, but he was sure she'd caught him staring. "Hey. Sorry. I just was passing and I thought...well, you didn't come in tonight.

Again. You didn't come in last week, either. I wanted to make sure you were okay."

As soon as he said it, he knew that was the truth. Sure his pride was stung that she seemed to be avoiding him, but he'd been a little worried, too. He watched her expression go from startled to suspicious.

"Why wouldn't I be?"

"Are you?" he asked, one hand on the freezing metal railing, one foot on the step. He could turn around and leave in a second if he had to. He hoped he didn't have to.

"I'm fine." She looked at the cider in his hand, then his bare fingers curled around the railing. "You're insane, it's twenty degrees out here. No gloves? No hat?"

"I run warm," he told her, although he was freezing. He hadn't planned for any kind of walk tonight.

"Get inside," Colleen commanded.

The tone of her voice heated him up, no question about that. Jesse inched past her, trying not to be a total creep and rub against her, though she was holding the door open for him and there wasn't much room for him to pass. In her living room, he made sure to stand carefully on the throw rug just inside the door to keep his messy boots from dirtying the hardwood floors. He held out the cider.

Colleen didn't take it. She closed the door, then crossed her arms to stare at him. "Why are you here, really?"

"I wanted to see you," he said. There wasn't any point in lying. Not now. "And since you obviously weren't going to come in and see me…"

She flinched a little, looking embarrassed for a second or so before her chin lifted. "You don't know that. Maybe I was busy. Or sick."

"That's why I came to see if you were all right." He grinned.

After a moment, she returned his smile, though not as brightly. "You brought... What is that? Hard cider? Not chicken soup. What if I really *was* sick?"

"But you're not."

"No," she said after a second. "But I like soup."

"So you were just avoiding me, then." The bottles clinked lightly as he shifted the six-pack to his other hand. "You know, I could go get you some soup. If you wanted some."

"You don't have to," she began, then stopped. "You know what? Yeah. I like soup, and I'm actually hungry. Go get me some soup, Jesse."

Her voice dipped on the syllables of his name. The sound of it sent a tickle of arousal up his spine, no good reason why. Just that his name from her mouth sounded thick and sensual and full of longing, and the sudden gleam in her eyes, the way she shifted from foot to foot, the puckering of her nipples so clear through her shirt, all told him that something in what she was asking of him was turning her on. At the thought of that, the crotch of his jeans grew tight.

"Yes, ma'am," he told her, and watched in aroused fascination as her lips parted.

Colleen swiped her lower lip with her tongue and stepped aside so he could move past her to the front door. "Leave the cider. It will be here when you get back."

He wasn't going to come back. Colleen had been stupid to send him out into the frigid night to buy what, soup? She let out a groan. Soup, for God's sake. First of all, where was Jesse even going to find soup at this time of night? Second, why hadn't she just told him to go and not come back? Hadn't she decided she wasn't going to see him again? She didn't need the aggravation.

That might be what her overactive mind told her, but it

wasn't what her body wanted. The second she'd figured out
the shadowy figure on her front steps was Jesse and not some
random stranger getting ready to bludgeon her to death and
steal her grandma's silver—or worse, Steve, stopping by "just
to check in" on her—her hormones had gone into overdrive.
She'd tossed out the comment about soup without thinking,
but the second he'd offered to do what she'd asked, time had
seemed to slow. Even to stand still for a second or so while her
breath caught up to the hammer of her heartbeat in her ears.

He would do what she wanted him to do, because she
asked.

And that had been enough to nearly send her to her knees,
which had reminded her swiftly of how easily Jesse had gone
to his, and after that, there was nothing left inside her but
the flames of desire consuming her. Then he'd actually gone
out the front door, leaving behind the hard cider she had no
urge to drink. Looking at the six-pack now, her stomach did
another slow, rolling tumble.

He wouldn't be back, she thought as she turned the shower
water to hot and stripped quickly out of her grungy pj's. He'd
be running as far and fast as he could in the opposite direc-
tion. But just in case, she was going to shave her legs. And
armpits. And...well, all the other pertinent places.

She got in the water before it was more than lukewarm,
teeth chattering, rushing to be sure she'd be finished in case
he did come back, which he wasn't going to do, of course.
But if he did, she thought as she ran the razor over her legs
and forced herself to slow down so she didn't cut herself, she
needed to be able to hear the door.

In less than ten minutes she'd finished. Smoothed lotion
over her damp, goose-bumpy skin. Blotted her face with
powder, dabbed on some gloss, added a bit of mascara. Nothing obvious. She didn't want him to know she'd made an ef-

fort. At the last minute, Colleen ran a damp brush through her hair, praying it wouldn't frizz. Then she slipped into a pair of silky pajama bottoms meant for summer wear, but far more flattering than the ancient flannels she'd been wearing. She looked in the mirror.

It would have to do.

She was downstairs when the front doorbell rang. For an eternal second, Colleen considered not answering the door, but it was close to ten-thirty now, and it could only be Jesse. He'd come back. Her stomach and her heart both fought to climb into her throat, but she forced a neutral expression as she opened the door.

His grin, though, that smile lit up his striking blue eyes and made everything about him shine. She couldn't ignore it. She had to return it.

"Hey." He held up a paper bag emblazoned with the name of one of the local restaurants. "Soup."

Sudden and embarrassing tears stung the backs of her eyes before she forced them away. Her chin went up, her smile fading. "What kind?"

"Chicken with dumplings."

Oh, shit. He did know her. She couldn't fathom how she had become so knowable to him, this man who was essentially a stranger, but he'd chosen the one item on that restaurant's menu that she'd ever ordered.

"I got enough for two," Jesse said. "I'm starving."

"Bring it back here." Without looking to see if he followed, Colleen went into the kitchen. She tried to tell herself the shivering came from her bare feet on the chilly tiles, but the truth was, she couldn't stop herself from shaking with fever heat at the thought of his mouth on hers, his hands all over her.

She put out glass bowls and spoons for each of them. She

stepped back from the table, watching him to see what he'd do. Jesse took the soup containers from the bag and emptied them into the bowls. Steam rose, curling lazily. He must've run here to keep them so warm, and more of her own heat rose inside her.

"Hungry?" Jesse gave her another of those grins.

"Yes," Colleen said. "But not for soup."

The electric arc of sexual tension snapped between them. In the next moment he'd crossed to her. Backed her up against the counter. Kissing, kissing, oh, damn, it felt so good to have his tongue in her mouth. His hand between her legs, fingers stroking just right through the silky fabric of her bottoms. Then he bent to her neck, scraping his teeth along her flesh, and she wanted to leap out of her skin from the pleasure of it.

"Take off my shirt." The words rasped out of her. "Get your mouth on me."

Jesse moaned softly and tugged her slim-fit, long-sleeved T-shirt over her head. Her nipples pebbled at once from the cold air and anticipation, but in the next moment the heated slickness of his mouth closed over first one and then the other, and she was anything but chilly. Her fingers sunk deep into the dark thickness of his hair, holding him close. He sucked gently, then a little harder. His hand moved against her, and his fingers moved up to dip inside the waistband.

Colleen stopped him, pulling his hair until he looked up at her. "No."

His glazed gaze cleared a little. He licked his lips. "No?"

"I want you to go upstairs and get undressed for me. I want you to..." Her breath caught. She faltered, stumbling, but at the sight of his expression, Colleen went calm. Steady. And oh, fuck, so turned on she thought she might not be able to make it up the stairs herself. "I want you to get on your knees, and I want that pretty cock so hard for me that it bounces on your belly when I come into the room. Do you want that, Jesse?"

He nodded.

"Answer me." She made the words hard, but not harsh.

"Yes, ma'am. I want to get on my knees for you."

Him calling her ma'am should've made her laugh. It should've made him sound like he was reading dialogue from a bad porn movie. But looking at him, all Colleen could think about was how easily he did it. How willingly.

"Go," she said.

He went. He knew where her bedroom was, of course. They'd spent enough time in it that last snowy weekend. She waited for the sound of his footsteps on the floorboards overhead, which was less familiar to her. When you lived alone, you didn't often hear the sound of your own floors creaking from below.

When she'd judged he'd had enough time to do as she'd requested, Colleen climbed the stairs. Her bedroom was at the far end. It had once been two small rooms, but the former owner had knocked down the wall between them to create a master suite. Jesse had left the door half-closed, and she hesitated before pushing it open. Not because she was afraid he wouldn't have done what she wanted him to do, but because seeing him on his knees, naked and waiting for her…the thought of it made it hard to breathe. Seeing it for real was going to be intense.

And oh, it was.

He'd done what she told him, all right. Stripped down to that tawny, naked flesh. On his knees next to the armchair she'd put catty corner by the window with a reading lamp. His arms were at his sides when she came through the door, but at once he put them behind his back. Back straight, shoulders squared. Head up. Cock hard.

She wanted to touch him and taste him, but first, Colleen wanted to look at him. She circled him, one hand lightly touching his hair. His shoulders. His chest. She traced the line of his collarbones and delighted in the way his cock did, indeed, bounce to tap his belly. When she dug her fingers into his hair and tipped his head back, he closed his eyes. Mouth open.

She kissed him, long and lingering, until they were both breathless. She reached to stroke him, remembering every inch as though it hadn't been two long and stupid weeks since she'd touched him this way. A slick, clear bead of precome slipped out of him, and she used her fingers to smooth it over the head of his cock.

Jesse groaned. "Oh…fuck. That feels good."

"I want you to feel good," she whispered. "I want you to come for me so hard. Are you going to come for me, Jesse?"

He swallowed and murmured, "Yes. Please."

She stroked him again. Up and down, fingers circling. His prick leaped in her hand, throbbing, and she gripped him at the base to keep him still. He was breathing hard, the skin of his cock going that lovely, delicious shade of aroused red. He opened his eyes to stare into hers, and she stroked him slowly, letting his slickness coat her hand. When he needed more, she held out her palm to him.

"Spit."

He did. It might have been disgusting, but both of them shuddered at the pool of clear fluid on her skin. When she reached to stroke him again, slippery now, he muttered what sounded like a plea.

"What's that?" she asked into his ear, her lips moving on his skin.

"Feels good," he said. "I'm close."

Colleen slowed her stroking to study him. This was power, she thought, mesmerized at the sight of his arousal and how willingly he'd given himself to her. Her pussy clenched at the thought of it, how her simple touch could send him to the edge so quickly.

She eased off, not letting go of him but simply no longer stroking. He groaned, hips pushing forward, but she gave him nothing. Her breathing quickened. Colleen shifted, feeling the pull of her pajama bottoms against her swollen clit. Another stroke had him shuddering, but again she stopped just before he tipped over the edge.

Colleen stood up straight, making sure Jesse was watching. She stripped, slowly but without fanfare, setting her clothes aside until she was naked in front of him, her nipples hard, her cunt, slick and aching to be filled.

"I want your mouth on me," she said in a low voice. "Just your mouth. Keep your hands behind your back."

It wasn't that she didn't want his hands. It was that having him obey her turned her on as much, if not more, than his fingers on her skin. She moved forward to give him access to her pussy, bending just enough to put her hands on his shoulders. Her legs spread, his mouth buried in her heat, she rocked her clit against Jesse's willing and eager tongue.

It wasn't going to take long. She'd been turned on since seeing him come through her front door, and her arousal had been building steadily the entire time. With his lips and tongue and oh, shit, teeth, his fucking teeth, working their magic on her flesh, Colleen was going to climax without much effort at all.

She cupped the back of his head to hold him to her as her hips moved helplessly. She didn't care about the awkwardness of the position, or that her calf muscles were starting to ache or that surely his knees had to be killing him by now. All that mattered right then was the pleasure spiraling up and up and up until she was suffused with the glory of mind-shattering ecstasy.

He cried out, muffled against her. Wet heat spurted against her thighs as he came, and this sent her over the edge again into another shuddering climax. He'd ejaculated without touching himself, shooting high enough to hit her, and purely from the pleasure of making her come. She thought her orgasm might never end, but at last it eased and left her breathless and weak-kneed. Colleen took a few unsteady steps back to let herself sink onto the edge of the bed. She cupped her pussy, feeling the aftershocks rippling through her.

Jesse looked stunned. Slickness glistened on his belly and chest, and she could still feel it sliding down her skin. She was sure she looked stunned, herself.

"I never," he began, but seemed incapable of saying more.

They looked at each other. Colleen let out a low, unexpected laugh. Jesse looked surprised, but in the next moment he'd started laughing, too. Oh, this was going to hurt so hard when it ended, she thought. It was going to slay her.

But it wasn't over yet.

CHAPTER SEVEN

"I had a dog when I was married." Colleen handed Jesse the box of canned food and supplies she'd helped him buy at the local pet supply store for his Saturday volunteer shift. "His name was Pete. He bit my ex-husband once."

Jesse closed the trunk of his car. "Ouch. Bet that made him angry."

"He'd been drinking and teasing the dog. You don't poke a dog without risking its teeth," she said with a shrug as she went around to get in on the passenger side.

Jesse got behind the wheel. "We always had dogs growing up. One of the first things I'm going to do once I can get into my own place is get a dog. Probably even foster some. It's good for kids to have pets."

Colleen adjusted her seat belt. "Can't you get a place that allows dogs?"

Jesse paused, then figured what the hell. There was no point in trying to pretend he wasn't broke most of the time. "Nothing I can afford. Not in Laila's school district or close enough to work to make it worthwhile."

"Oh." Colleen looked uncomfortable, which hadn't been his intention. "Sorry."

"Don't be sorry. I've got a dozen pooches waiting for me at the shelter," Jesse replied lightly.

He reached to hold her hand as they drove, letting his thumb rub the back of it. Her skin was so soft. He wanted to hold her hand forever.

At the shelter, he showed her where to put the supplies, then took her into the back room where the rescue dogs that hadn't yet been put up for adoption were kept. Five today, ranging from puppy to senior dog. All had been taken from abusive homes. Some were recovering from surgeries or injuries.

"This old girl here, this is Sasha." Jesse led Colleen to the quiet black-and-white mutt in the corner. "She's friendly but skittish. But if you give her time, she'll give you plenty of love. She wants to be a lapdog."

Colleen bent to let Sasha sniff her fingers. "Hey, sweet girl."

Together, Jesse and Colleen spent an hour or so grooming and giving the dogs the love and attention they'd been missing. Then another hour cleaning pens and putting away donated supplies. He'd been concerned she might find the work too dirty or boring, but the time passed with them laughing and joking the entire time. Even singing. She had a terrible voice and was very proud of it.

"Surprised the dogs aren't howling," she said when she'd finished a verse of some pop song that had been getting constant airplay.

Jesse took the chance to pull her into his arms. "What did you do with the money?"

"What money?" Colleen pushed up on her toes to brush her mouth to his.

"The money I gave you for—"

"Singing lessons," she said along with him, then swatted him. "Jerk."

He laughed and pulled her close again. They were alone in the supply closet, so he took another chance. The kiss was sweet but had the promise of heat. She broke it first with a small, self-conscious laugh.

"Thanks for coming with me today." Jesse kept his hands on her hips.

Colleen smiled. "Thanks for asking me. It's good to give back to something. You know?"

"Yeah. I think so." He wanted to kiss her again, but held off, not wanting to push it. "Hey, you hungry? I promised you dinner."

"You did. And I am." She backed up as much as the small space allowed. "Are we finished here?"

He nodded, trying to think of a reason to stay with her in the closet long enough to steal another kiss, but unable to find one that wouldn't be totally transparent. "Just let me put my name on the schedule for next week, and we're good to go."

He'd thought a lot about where to take her, wishing someplace fancy like Fogo de Chão was in his budget instead of a local dive diner, but Nancy's Hot Spot had the best steak and eggs he'd ever tasted, no matter what time of day you went. They made a pretty good gyro, too.

"Hope it's okay," he said as they slid into one of the cracked red vinyl booths toward the back.

Before Colleen had a chance to answer, the tiny woman with a towering dome of teased crimson hair came to give him a hug and a kiss. Without asking, she poured them both mugs of steaming coffee. "Hey, hon. Good to see ya. Where's the little one?"

"Laila is with her mom today. This is Colleen. Colleen, this is Nancy." Jesse grinned as Colleen made the connection.

"Nancy's Hot Spot Nancy?" She looked around. "This is your place?"

"Been for 'bout forty years or so. Yep." Nancy poked Jesse's arm. "The usual, hon?"

"Steak and eggs. Sunny-side up. Hash browns. And a biscuit."

Colleen oohed. "I'll take the same. And coffee, obviously."

"Sounds like a match made in heaven." Nancy winked and headed off to put their orders in.

"This place is great." Colleen added cream and sugar to her cup and sipped. "Coffee's good, too."

"I love this place. I started working here in high school. Nancy made sure I did my homework during the slow times and that I also picked up enough hours to help make ends meet when Laila was just born. I owe her a lot. She keeps trying to talk me into buying the restaurant, but I haven't been able to get together the cash to make her an offer I wouldn't be ashamed of." Jesse pushed another sugar packet toward her, noticing she'd only used two.

Colleen paused before picking it up, but then tore the paper and dumped the sugar into her coffee. "You want to own a diner?"

"Yeah." He looked around, then back at her. "Yeah, I think so. I've thought about a bar, but...yeah, I'd like to own a diner."

She smiled. "I'd never have guessed it about you."

"Now you know."

They stared at each other across the table without saying anything. They didn't have to. It was easy being with her.

They stayed at that diner for another two hours, covering all sorts of topics. They challenged each other to the tic-tac-toe games printed on the front of the place mats, each of them winning one game and Colleen taking the third. She'd polished off her entire plate of food, matching him bite for bite, which was impressive and a little intimidating, since she was only half his size.

"This is one of the best dates I have ever had," he told her sincerely when they were back in the car heading for her place so he could drop her off. Night had fallen, and the air promised more snow, even if the weather report wasn't calling for any.

Colleen twisted in her seat to look at him. "This was a date?"

"Well…yeah." He pulled into the spot he'd cleared for her, glad the plows had come through to open up the rest of the street, and turned off the ignition. He twisted toward her. "You didn't think so?"

She bit her lower lip for a second. "I wasn't sure."

"I could've made it fancier, huh?" He gave her a hang-dog look that fortunately made her laugh, which was what he was going for.

"No. This was great. I had a great time. It's also one of the best dates I've ever had," she told him. She paused, then said, "It's been a long time since I went on a date. I guess I wasn't thinking of it that way. Because…well…"

Because they'd slept together already? Or because he was a bartender who couldn't afford an apartment that allowed dogs? Or because he'd taken her to a diner instead of a fancy Brazilian steak place? Jesse didn't want to ask.

"Come inside with me," Colleen said suddenly, and then it no longer mattered what she'd meant.

Jesse was in her living room. Again. After a date, no less. Of course it had been a date. Why else would he have taken her to the shelter, then to eat? Colleen thought. It wasn't like they were…friends.

She already knew how he tasted and smelled and the sound of his voice when he cried out during an orgasm. Now she knew so much more about him, and though she tried as hard as she could to think of something she didn't like, there hadn't been one thing today that had turned her off. If anything, the more time she spent with him, the better she liked him.

It was disgruntling.

"I don't have anything stronger. Sorry." She handed him a glass of brewed iced tea.

Jesse had made himself at home on her couch. He took the glass and set it on the table, on a coaster even. "That's okay. Just because I work in a bar doesn't mean I always have to have booze. This is good, actually."

"I don't drink," Colleen said.

He smiled. "Yeah. I know. Except maybe once every long while, huh?"

Embarrassment stung the back of her neck and tips of her ears. "Kind of proved my point, didn't it?"

"I don't know," Jesse said. "What's the point?"

"You mean why I sit every Thursday night with a glass of whiskey and don't drink it?" Colleen put her own glass on the table next to his and took a seat on the couch, though she kept a distance between them.

"The question had crossed my mind, yeah." Jesse leaned forward to put his elbows on his knees, hands clasped. His gaze was earnest. Sincere. Open.

She didn't want to tell him.

"It's a way to prove something to myself, I guess. That I don't need it."

His brow furrowed. "Okay?"

"Thursday nights were the start of the weekend when I lived with my ex. He'd come home from work and have a beer or two while I got ready to go." She paused, thinking. "Even if I was all ready to go. And then we'd go out to one of his favorite places. Usually Doc's, but sometimes we'd have dinner, too. He was a fun drunk on Thursday nights. By Sunday afternoon, he was usually hurting and not as much fun."

To give him credit, Jesse didn't look appalled. He didn't

look too surprised, either. He probably saw a lot of that sort of drinking at The Fallen Angel. It wouldn't even faze him, she thought, but that didn't make the memories any easier.

"And you?" he asked carefully.

"I drank with him. To keep him company, at first. And then because he liked to tell me that I needed to loosen up and have a few so that I wasn't so uptight. He was right about that, I guess. At least the more I drank, the easier it was to be with him." She took a drink of iced tea, though she wasn't thirsty. She gave Jesse a sideways look. "After a while, it got hard to tell if I drank to get along with him, or because I needed it as much as he did. That I needed booze to keep me from being uptight and controlling. Because having control and being controlling aren't the same thing."

"I know that."

"So…I come in on Thursday nights and order that whiskey to prove to myself that I don't need it. I don't even really want it. And that night, that first night with you…"

"You drank it then."

"I was upset," she told him. "Steve had said some things that really hit home. You know how some people know exactly how to get to you? A word or two, right where it hurts?"

He nodded.

"Well, he did that to me, and I went to the Angel thinking I was going to let him win. I was going to drink and get loose and be everything he'd said I was. I don't know why. I was worn down, I guess." She frowned, hating herself for that. "I was stupid."

"You are anything but stupid." He reached for her hand, and she let him take it.

His fingers were strong and warm, and she couldn't help thinking about how he'd made her feel when he touched her. With a shaky breath, Colleen squeezed his hand. "You barely know me."

"I could get to know you." He moved closer.

Then he was kissing her, which was what she'd wanted him to do all day long. Colleen opened her mouth for him, inviting his tongue. When he gave it to her, she put her hand on the back of his neck to hold him close. They kissed and kissed and kissed, until both were breathing hard and she had to pull away to get some air.

"You're an amazing kisser, Colleen."

Her first instinct was to scoff, but something stopped her. "I know."

He didn't laugh, which was good because she hadn't been making a joke. With Jesse, she felt like an amazing kisser. She felt amazing, period.

He pushed some hair off her forehead, then let his hand rest on her shoulder. "I had a great time with you today."

"I know," she repeated softly, inching closer.

"You're a lot of fun," Jesse whispered as she fit herself against him. "You're smart. And pretty. And so damned sexy."

"I know, I know, I know," Colleen continued and kissed him long and hard.

"I want to touch you."

She smiled into his mouth. "I know."

"I want to be inside you."

Her breath hitched, cracking her answer, but even though the words were garbled, she was sure he understood them. "I...know."

"Tell me to go, if you want me to, but..."

"Upstairs," she told him. "Take me upstairs, Jesse, and fuck me until we both forget how to walk."

CHAPTER EIGHT

"You're in a good mood," Diane observed, lifting an eyebrow. A familiar expression. She'd known Jesse for so long, yet seemed continuously capable of being surprised by the things he did.

He waited until Laila disappeared up the steps into his apartment before answering. "Had a good night."

Diane, to give her credit, did not roll her eyes. She looked past him to make sure their daughter was out of hearing range, too. "What's her name?"

"Can't hide anything from my girls, can I?" Jesse reached to poke her arm, but Diane danced out of the way.

She frowned. Shit, she was upset? She never got jealous about his dates.

"I'm not your girl, obviously. So it *is* a woman. Laila said you had a new girlfriend."

"I don't. Yet." Jesse eyed her, wondering how his daughter had figured it out and chalking it up to the fact she was genius-level smart. "But maybe I will, if I'm lucky."

What's it to you? was the unspoken question that would remain unsaid, because to put it into words would sound belligerent. It would prompt a fight, and he didn't want that. Jesse shivered in the cold air, too aware of his bare feet and chest. He'd come down to answer the door in only a pair of jeans. He'd barely made it home in time to shower before it was time for Diane to drop off Laila, and by the way she was looking him over, he was guessing she'd figured that out.

"Edward and I are having some trouble," Diane said. "That's all."

Jesse frowned. "Oh. Sorry to hear that."

"Laila is going to take it hard if we break up, Jesse."

"That bad, huh?" He meant the breakup, not his daughter's reaction to it. He had an idea that Laila would be better about it than Diane expected.

"She needs stability." Diane shot another glance over his shoulder. "Consistency. I'm just saying now might not be the best time for you to bring in someone new."

It was his turn for an eyebrow lift. In the beginning, when they'd been kids trying to figure out how to be parents, he and Diane had argued a lot over stupid things. When they'd finally parted as a couple, agreeing it was better to be friends who raised a child together than enemies who ruined one, they'd still argued, but it had been about different stupid stuff. They'd never, however, argued about who they were dating. Or when to date someone.

"It's still early. You know I don't bring just anyone around, Diane."

"Well, you're obviously fucking this new woman, whoever she is."

Jesse bit back a retort and made sure to keep his voice calm. "And?"

"Nothing." Diane drew in a deep breath and gave him an insincere smile. "I'm sure you'll do the right thing."

Annoyed now, Jesse stepped back into the foyer to get out of the cold. "You make that sound like a question."

"I'm upset. Forget it. Sorry. I know you'll take our daughter's best interests into account when you decide what's more important, her welfare or your dick."

"Wow," Jesse said after those words had hung in the air between them for a few seconds. "Well, then, you have a great day."

She gave him a bitter, brittle smile and left him standing there in the cold.

"I've never seen it." Colleen cradled her phone to her ear as she stirred the pot of noodles and got ready to drain them. "I've seen most of the others, but not the newer ones."

"We have the whole Disney collection. A bunch of VHS tapes, even. Totally old-school." Jesse's voice was pitched low because he was with his daughter watching *The Fox and the Hound*.

Colleen had told him to enjoy the time with Laila, that he didn't have to be on the phone with her, but she was still blushingly pleased that he wanted to talk to her badly enough to make it a priority even when he had other stuff going on. "Wow. I don't even have a VCR anymore."

"I pick them up at yard sales and thrift stores. You know, some of them can be worth a lot of money, actually. Not that I'm buying them to sell. Just to enjoy."

She heard a shuffling, and the sound of the movie got far away. Then all she heard was the soft in-out huff of his breathing. "What's going on?"

"Came into my bedroom to talk to you in private."

Colleen pressed the phone to her ear and closed her eyes for a moment, unable to stop her grin. Why did something so simple make her so happy? She wanted to shake it off, but let herself indulge in the glow a little longer. He wanted to talk to her. He wanted her.

Still… "I should let you go."

"No, no, it's fine. She's totally into the movie. It's our Friday night thing. Disney and Chinese food." Jesse sounded like he was smiling, too. "We've got a good one coming up, *The Sword in the Stone*. Mad Madam Mim. You'd like it."

They'd talked every day, sometimes only a few texts, sometimes a few hours of conversation. She'd sent him a list of commands, intrigued to see what he'd do with them, and had been sent spiraling into heady, giddy arousal when he'd returned her text with detailed descriptions, including photos, of exactly how he'd fulfilled her demands. They'd been in near-constant communication, yet she hadn't actually seen him since last week.

She'd suggested dinner on his night off, but he'd had his daughter with him. And though she could've gone in to see him at The Fallen Angel during his shift, Colleen didn't want to be that woman, the one who hung around all starry-eyed about her lover while he tried to do his job. And because he slept during the day and she worked outside the city, lunch had been out of the question.

"I miss you," she said impulsively. "I wish I could see you tonight."

"Yeah… Me, too. But I have Laila."

It was too soon for her to meet his child, even for something as casual as Disney and Chinese. She knew that. And frankly, the idea of meeting Jesse's daughter was more than a little intimidating. It was a bigger step toward something Colleen was still trying to convince herself wasn't going to happen. Yet it had been almost a week since she'd seen him. Touched him.

"Right. I didn't mean I expected to. I just meant I wanted to, Jesse."

Her voice dipped, going raspy and low. They'd had phone sex two nights before, a first for her, and he'd told her afterward that it had been the way she said his name that had finally tipped him over the edge. She couldn't hear herself say it now without remembering that.

Before he could answer, her phone beeped. She looked at the number, wincing when she saw it was Steve. If she didn't answer she'd only have to call him back.

"I'm getting a call," she told Jesse. "Can I call you back when I'm done?"

He hesitated. "Yeah…I mean, I might be busy. But sure."

Colleen hesitated, too, cursing Steve's timing. "I know you're with your daughter, Jesse. If you don't want me to call you—"

"No. It's okay. It's fine. Call me back."

Something was off in his tone, but she disconnected the call anyway. It was too late to catch Steve, so she dialed him back without listening to his voice mail. Consequently, when he answered brusquely, she was instantly wary and wishing she'd warned herself.

"What are you, a moron?" Steve said.

Colleen bit back a caustic reply. "Nice."

"It's not that hard, you know," Steve told her. "To make sure someone's at the house to handle deliveries and repairs. That's a necessary thing, Colleen, about having a property you don't live in. Someone to take care of it."

She had someone who looked after the property, and Steve knew it, but she didn't point it out. Arguing with him was pointless, because nobody won against Steve. Steve was never wrong. Steve was never sorry. Steve was never responsible.

Steve, Colleen thought, could go fuck himself.

"What were you having delivered?"

"Some things for the house," he said impatiently. "Obviously."

Though she'd trained herself to listen for the sound of slurring in his voice that meant he'd been drinking, she also knew he'd been on the wagon for a year now. It hadn't done much for his temperament. He'd been easier to please when he was drunk, and being dry had only made him more self-righteous and cranky.

"What things? Also, Steve, you know Joe takes care of the house in the winter. You could've called him yourself."

"How was I supposed to know?"

She grimaced. "Because he's done it for years? Who did you think would be there to take your delivery? I mean, nobody lives there, Steve. Did you imagine somehow it might magically happen on its own? And what repairs are you talking about?"

"I broke a window the last time I was down."

At this, she paused, choosing her words carefully. "How did that happen?"

"I was locked out. I was trying to get in." Same old Steve, sounding stubborn. "You didn't leave the key in the right place the last time you were there."

She hadn't been there in months, too busy with work and the bad weather to think about getting away for a weekend, though she loved the beach in winter, maybe even more than during the summer. Steve's casual blame rubbed her like sandpaper. "I absolutely did. And I haven't been there since October."

It didn't matter what she said. Whatever had happened was her fault. It always was, and she was sick of it.

"Don't expect me to pay for the window," she told him briskly. "Or for whatever it was you ordered for the house.

You know we're supposed to agree on everything before we do it. Like we're supposed to consult each other on scheduling visits."

"Right. Because you just have to have your say." His voice dripped with derision that once would've had her hot with guilt. "Have to be in charge, right? In control of everything."

"Fuck you, Steve."

He made a startled noise but recovered quickly. "No, thanks, sweetheart... Your cunt has teeth."

Colleen disconnected before he could continue with what she knew would be something harsh and crude. When he called back, she sent him directly to voice mail. Breathing hard, her world spun. She paced, fury fisting her hands hard enough for her fingernails to cut into her palms.

She was done letting him make her feel bad, she told herself. Steve was not her lover. Not a friend. He was an arrogant, pathetic tyrant who'd never learned the art of getting along with other people.

And once, long ago, she had loved him.

Colleen's knees gave out, and she sank onto the couch to put her head in her hands. Steve, when they met, had been charming and affable and considerate. He'd been funny. He'd made her feel pretty and wanted and important, at least for a time, until the years had passed and things had changed. She'd never really been sure exactly why or how, or what she'd done to cause it, or how she might've prevented it. Remembering how she'd felt about him in the beginning only made her feel so much worse about how much she disliked him now.

Her phone buzzed again with another call from him. Again, she sent it to voice mail. He could berate her until his heart's content and she could delete the message without listening to it. She could delete his texts unread. She didn't need to tolerate his abuse any longer, not even for the sake of once having been in love.

Still, her heart pounded and her palms hurt. Her jaw ached from clenching it. Her face felt hot. She picked up her phone and dialed a number that had become familiar.

"Jesse," she said. "I need you."

CHAPTER NINE

"Laila's asleep." Jesse scooted the popcorn bowl out of the way so he could sit a little closer to Colleen on the couch.

He couldn't stop himself from brushing away the heavy length of her hair that had fallen over her shoulder. Mindful of what Diane had said, he hadn't intended to invite Colleen over. He'd been trying to keep at least a little bit of distance this week for Laila's sake. The kid hadn't even mentioned Diane's split with Edward, and when he'd tried to gently bring up the subject, she'd given him a blank sort of look and a shrug. Colleen wouldn't have been the first girlfriend Jesse had ever brought around, though it had been a couple years since there'd been anyone special enough to introduce to his kid. It had made sense to take a step back to consider what Diane had said, but clearly it wasn't an issue.

And Colleen had said she needed him.

He'd been lost to her, then. Her need, an aphrodisiac. His desire to please her, undeniable.

Colleen put her head on his shoulder and nuzzled into him. It had only been a little over a month since the weekend of the snowstorm, but everything about her felt as though he'd known her forever. Her hair tickled his nose, but he didn't move until he felt the whisper of her lips on his throat. Then he couldn't stop himself from twitching.

She laughed against him. "Stay still."

"Yes, ma'am."

He felt a moment of tension in her, but it faded immediately. She spoke against his skin, letting her teeth press him now and then. "I like it when you say that. Too much."

"Why too much?" His hands roamed her back, stopping just above the sweet curve of her ass. Waiting for her to urge him with her body to touch her there.

"All of this is too much," he thought she said, but her voice had dipped so low he couldn't be sure of her words.

When she moved against him, pushing his shoulders to the back of the couch so she could straddle him, then take his face in her hands, Jesse's head tipped back. Colleen nudged his chin to tip it farther, exposing the line of his throat to her hungry, nibbling mouth. She rocked on his lap, and he was rock-hard in seconds. That was what she did to him. A word, a look, a touch, and he was aching for her.

It was more than the sex. It was her laughter when he teased her. The softness of her breathing when she fell asleep curled inside the circle of his arms. How she looked in the morning, rumpled from sleep, so sexy and sweet and delicious.

He was falling for her in a big way, and nothing had made that more evident than how he'd felt this entire week without seeing her…and how he'd felt the moment he saw her tonight.

She kissed his mouth, hard and bruising, and caught his lower lip between her teeth, tugging. She stopped before it really hurt, then used the sweetness of her tongue to lick away the ache. She ground herself against him, her soft, heavy tits crushing to his chest until he wanted to thrust hard against her. But he didn't.

Because she hadn't said for him to move.

Jesse'd known for a long time what flipped his switch. He'd dated a girl who'd been really into camping. Tying knots. She'd had her own collection of ropes for climbing, and though he'd never taken up the sport, he'd gained a true appreciation for all the uses of carabiner clips and smooth nylon cord. It had never occurred to him that what he liked was submission, though later internet porn had taught him some kinky new terms to describe what got him off.

"Open," she demanded of his mouth, and he gave it to her. Her tongue stroked his. Then she sucked his gently before breaking the kiss to breathe. "You taste so good."

His fingers tightened on her hips. He wanted to slide his hands beneath her shirt, but kept himself from it. She must've seen it in his face, though, because she gave him a curious half-tilting smile.

"You want to touch me."

"Oh, yeah. Yes." He tried, teasing the hem of her shirt upward to get at the smooth heat of her skin, judging to see if she was going to let him…or if she'd get stern. Either was a win, as far as he was concerned.

"Tell me, Jesse, what you want to do to me?"

That stumped him for a moment. "You want me to talk dirty?"

"I want you to tell me what you want to do to me," Colleen said into his ear before taking his lobe in her teeth and biting. When he reacted with a groan, her low and throaty laugh tickled his ear and sent another surge of arousal straight to his skyward-pointing cock. "And how it makes you feel. Describe it to me."

Shit. He wasn't that great with words. But she hadn't asked, she'd commanded, and there was no way he was going to disappoint her if he could help it.

"I want to touch your tits," he breathed, arching his back when she ground harder onto his dick. "Take them in my hands and flick your nipples tight and hard, and I want to put my mouth on them. Suck them until I hear you moan my name. Just keep sucking and licking them until they're swollen and hard and you can't stop yourself from moving against me."

Colleen's lips moved on his ear, but the rest of her had gone still. "More."

"I want to move down your body, between your legs, and settle in there. My mouth on you, making you moan my name."

She did when he said that, whispering it low. Jesse arched, thrusting upward, helpless not to move at the sound of her voice. Colleen cupped his face, looking into his eyes. Then slowly, deliberately, she slid back a little on his thighs to un-buckle his jeans. She freed him with some struggle, but in a minute his cock was in her mouth, her hand at the base of it and stroking in tandem with the movement of her lips on his shaft.

It was his turn to mutter her name. His turn to dig his fingers into the fall of her hair. She felt so good, he couldn't do anything but let her have her wicked way with him.

Her stroking fingers moved to caress his balls, then a little lower. Jesse arched again, trying desperately not to thrust too hard, trying to wait for her commands. At the sound of her low chuckle, heat flooded him, but he couldn't keep himself from rolling his hips to get himself deeper into her mouth.

He looked down at her to see her meeting his gaze. "Col-leen, I'm close."

"Good." She bent back to him, sucking and licking, flicking her tongue along the underside of his cock until he thought he might die from it.

Over and over again she teased him to the edge and then slowed or stopped entirely while her hand kept a firm grip around him. He lost himself in the sight of her and in the pleasure building, building. Until at last he couldn't stand it anymore.

"I'm gonna—"

"Yes" was all she said, then bent back to him.

Jesse came hard enough to see stars. When he was able to open his eyes, he found Colleen giving him a very self-satisfied grin. She climbed onto his lap again to kiss him.

"Wow," he said.

"Hot," she answered.

They sat that way in silence for a few seconds. The pattern of their breathing aligned. So did the thump of their hearts. He pressed his face to the sweetness of her neck.

"Stay with me."

She nuzzled against him before pulling away. "I'm not sure I feel right having a sleepover with Laila here."

"She's okay with it," Jesse said. "Despite what her mother thinks."

Ah, shit, he'd screwed up again.

Colleen got off him to sit next to him on the couch, buttoning her jeans, which he hadn't noticed were undone. "What does her mother think?"

He reached for her hand. She let him take it but didn't squeeze when he did. "Just that since she's dumping her boyfriend, I shouldn't be getting a new girlfriend because it'll be disruptive to Laila. Which is just bullshit."

Colleen was silent. Her fingers untangled from his. She tucked her hands in her lap.

"Is that what I am? Your girlfriend?"

Jesse ran a fingertip down her arm, stopping at her wrist and letting his hand rest on his own thigh when she made no move to take it. "Do you want to be?"

She didn't answer him.

"Look, my kid's the most important thing in the world to me. I don't do stuff that I know will hurt her." Jesse frowned, watching Colleen's neutral expression. "But you know it's important for her to see that her parents have lives. And more important, that I can have a relationship that works and doesn't take anything away from my relationship with her. I don't want her to grow up thinking that the only way to love someone is by giving up everything else."

"Let me ask you something. Were you avoiding me this week? Seeing me, I mean."

"A little. Yes. I thought it was the right thing to do. But I was wrong!" he added hastily at the sight of her face. "Colleen, wait. I was wrong."

"When did you figure that out?"

"The minute you walked in the door tonight, and I realized that I'd been missing you all week like a part of me was gone," he told her honestly.

"But you weren't going to invite me over tonight."

He shook his head, hating the way this conversation was going. "No. I wasn't."

"What changed your mind?" she asked, looking into his eyes, her own bright. Her cheeks were flushed.

He had to tell her the truth; there was nothing else to say. "You told me you needed me."

Colleen got off the couch. "I'm going to go."

"Wait, what? No." Jesse got up, too, tucking himself quickly into his jeans and zippering them. "Colleen, don't go."

"I think it's better if I do. I'm not comfortable spending the night with your kid here." She didn't meet his gaze.

Jesse snagged her sleeve as she tried to duck away from him, but when she yanked herself from his grip, her eyes wide and mouth grim, he stepped back with his hands in the air. "Sorry."

"I had fun with you. But that's all it is. Fun." Colleen found her coat on the back of the chair and shrugged into it. "Your kid seems great, but maybe her mother is right. Maybe this isn't the right time for you to have a girlfriend."

"Or maybe you're just not the right girlfriend. Is that it?" He regretted the words as soon as he said them, but he knew at once by the way she looked at him that he'd hit the nail on the head.

Colleen tucked her scarf into her collar and put on her gloves. "Yes. Maybe that's it."

"Don't go," Jesse said to her when she was at the door leading to the stairs down to the street. "Please, Colleen. At least, not like this."

"Like what?" she asked without turning. "Look. I never made you any promises. I never tried to make you think…"

"Think what? That you liked me?"

Her shoulders squared, but she still wouldn't look back. "This was a mistake. I don't want to miss you when we aren't together. I don't want to need you."

"But you do," he said without trying to hide the bitterness in his voice.

She left, closing the door quietly behind her.

CHAPTER TEN

Jesse'd been given the blowoff before. More than once. Hell, a couple times he'd been flat out told to his face that his presence was no longer required. He kind of preferred that to the cold shoulder. Or ghosting. When a girl did that, just disappeared from his inbox, unfriending or no longer answering his texts, he hated that shit, too. Yet right now he'd have preferred to have at least the pretense that someday, maybe, Colleen would call him again. The thought of never seeing her again, never talking to her again, was just too fucking painful.

He'd called her, too stupid not to. She hadn't answered. He'd left messages that she hadn't returned. He'd sent texts, also ignored. She'd shut him out completely, and it was kind of killing him. At the same time, if that was what she wanted, his fucked up way of thinking meant that he had to give it to her. If she didn't want to need him, then all he could do was let her go.

"Dad!"

He hadn't been paying attention to Laila, but now turned his focus to the work sheet she was showing him. Jesse had never been good at reading or writing. Math had come easy to him. Math was numbers, which always added up the same way, unlike words, which could be spelled the same and mean different things, or the other way around. Laila was showing him a list of sentences she needed to do something with. What, he wasn't sure.

"You have to pick out the subject and object," his daughter said patiently, her pencil tapping.

"Your mom would be much better at this." Jesse scratched his chin beneath the stubble of a beard he'd been letting go for the past couple days.

"Too bad she's not here." Ah. This kid. Totally his, not that he'd ever doubted it. From the moment of her birth when she'd opened those eyes and squalled, he'd known he'd had a part in making her.

Jesse leaned to lightly smack the back of her head. "Wiseass."

"Look it up on the computer." Laila grinned without shame, showing him a smile so much like Diane's it gave his heart a little pang. She was going to be a heartbreaker in a year or so, and he wasn't looking forward to that at all.

"You look it up." Jesse pulled out his phone to check for messages he knew wouldn't be there.

"Dad!"

"Sorry, kid. I'm useless with this stuff." Jesse tucked away his phone and bent back to the work sheet. "Can you get a friend to help? Or wait for your mom?"

Laila shook her head. "It's due tomorrow."

And she was spending the night with him, since Diane had gone away on a business trip that Jesse suspected had more to do with the fact she'd replaced Edward with that guy from her office than an actual, necessary overnight stay. He didn't begrudge her or anything like that. Laila spent more time with her mother, and Diane deserved a break to get her freak on, even if she was being hypocritical about it. But it was stuff like this homework assignment that made Jesse feel like a failure as a dad, and that was never cool.

"Okay. Let's figure this out."

Two hours later, they'd finished up the homework, made some popcorn and settled in front of the TV to catch up on streaming episodes of *Perfect Strangers*. Laila couldn't get enough of crazy Balki and his belabored cousin Larry. And Jesse couldn't get enough of this time with his kid, who was growing up too fast. That didn't stop him from playing around on his phone, though, while they watched.

Colleen didn't have a Connex account, or if she did, she had it locked down so private he couldn't find it. She didn't tweet or post to PicStream, and a search of her name brought up thousands of results. Switching his search to images only, Jesse told himself it wasn't creepy or stalkery to be doing this, even as he made sure to keep his phone shielded from the too-curious eyes of his precocious kid.

Laila wasn't fooled, though. "Who is she?"

Caught, Jesse swiped his phone's screen to erase his business. "Who? Nobody. What?"

"You're checking out a lady." Laila scooped a handful of unpopped kernels and let them roll around in her mouth to suck off the butter and salt, unconcerned that she might choke on them. Or at the very least, crack a tooth.

Jesse held up the bowl. "Get rid of that mess. Your mom will kill me if you break your teeth."

"Ugh, Dad, c'mon." She bent to spit into the bowl anyway. She eyed him through the fringe of her sandy hair. "So, who is she?"

"Nobody."

"Is she the one you've been spending all that time with?

Is she the friend whose house you were at when you got snowed in?"

"I can't put one over on you, huh?" Jesse frowned. "Yeah. We've been spending time together."

"I knew it was a lady! Is she your girlfriend?" Laila's eyes gleamed, and she got up on her knees on the couch.

"No, Laila. She's not my girlfriend." The truth sucked.

"But you like her a lot?" Laila narrowed her eyes to look him over.

Jesse snorted softly. "I barely know her."

"So how come you're looking her up on the internet? Why didn't you just ask her if you could text her? Girls like it when you just ask." She said this so nonchalantly that Jesse was reminded again how different things were for kids now. And again how much trouble he was in for with this kid.

"I did text her," he admitted. "She didn't answer me. That's her way of saying no, I guess."

Laila scoffed. "To you?"

"Yeah. To me. Hey, kiddo, it's getting late. You should get ready for bed." Jesse took the bowl and stood, but Laila stopped him.

"If you really like her, you should tell her, Dad. That's what Mom says. She says when you really like somebody there's no point in waiting to tell them, because if you don't, someone else will."

"Your mom's full of good advice."

"She says Barry told her he liked her right away, and that's how she knew she should give him a shot," Laila added.

Jesse tried not to laugh, which would offend her. "Barry, huh? That guy she works with? You like him okay?"

"He's okay." She shrugged and got off the couch. "He's got a big TV and all the cable stations. And a cat."

"Ah. He sounds great."

Laila launched herself at him, almost spilling the popcorn kernels as she squeezed him. "He's not you, Dad. Don't worry."

Okay, so maybe he'd worried. Just the tiniest bit. Now he squeezed her back and tugged her ponytail. "Go get ready for bed."

She was right, he thought later as he cleaned up the kitchen from dinner and paid some bills. The wind gusted hard outside, reminding him that winter wasn't over yet. There were more storms coming, for sure. And if he wanted to spend any of them stranded with Colleen again, he'd better figure out a way to make that happen. At least he had to try.

But when Thursday rolled around again, no matter how many times he looked up at the jingle of the bell over The Fallen Angel's door announcing a new arrival, none of the customers were her.

"You look like shit."

Leave it to Mark to be so blunt, Colleen thought as she poured herself a mug of coffee she didn't want, but would drink anyway because what she really wanted was a doughnut. Mondays, Mondays. Ugh. "Gee, thanks."

"Seriously." He leaned too close for social propriety, almost like he wanted to sniff her. Or lick her. Either way, it was too close.

Colleen stepped back. "I'm tired. That's all. Haven't been sleeping."

"Ah. Up too late?" Mark grinned, showing all his teeth. He made a dirty gesture with one hand. "New guy?"

Her lack of sleep was certainly none of Mark's business, even if he'd always had a way of worming out the most personal details of her life. "Old guy, actually."

"Steve's been bothering you?"

She shrugged, not wanting to admit how Steve still managed to get under her skin. She'd managed to ignore him for a week, until he sent her flowers and an apology. She hated the flowers and didn't believe for a second he was sorry about anything, but dammit, she didn't want him doing anything to the beach house she didn't know about.

The past two days it had been nitpickery of the highest order. He was all over her about changing the rental management company, claiming they were the reason he'd needed to break the window. He wanted to fire Joe. He wanted to raise the summer rental rates and offer more weeks, which would mean less time there for both of them even if it meant more income. It was stupid stuff, pointless and done solely, she knew, to get under her skin. He'd also started needling her about updating the decor.

"Tell him to take a long walk off a short pier," Mark suggested. "That's what I told my last ex-wife when she wouldn't leave me alone."

Colleen frowned. "It's not that simple, and you know it."

Mark could be arrogant and wacky and inappropriate; he was also incredibly astute. "Come into my office."

"I have a client at four—"

"Now."

With a sigh, Colleen followed him into his office, where he waved her onto one of the weirdly squishy chairs in front of his desk. She cupped her mug in both hands, warming them. With the harsh winter they'd been having, Mark's office had become almost impossible to keep above sixty-five degrees.

"Look. What's it gonna take for you to boot him out of your life altogether? Get moving on? Start dating, for crying out loud? Beautiful woman like you, sleeping alone? *No bueno.* I'd have a go at you myself if I didn't think it would get us both in all kinds of trouble."

"Totally inappropriate," Colleen scolded, but she smiled.

"So quit." Mark sat back in his chair and propped his feet on the desk, his hands behind his head. "Walk out. Leave me and all this behind. Forge onward!"

She'd thought about quitting more than once, though she knew there was no way she would. Mark had given her this job when she needed to escape from a bad situation, and he'd done it to help her, not because she was qualified. No matter how she'd proven herself in the interim, she could never forget that.

"You don't need me, you know," Mark said. "You could go work anywhere."

His words touched that soft and rotten place inside her that shamed her even as it formed a big part of her core. Her smile faded. "I know that."

"This is a terrible place to work."

It wasn't. It was weird, and Mark was hard to work for sometimes, but she'd had worse jobs. She shook her head in silence.

"Steve's an asshole, Colleen."

"Tell me something I don't know."

Mark stared at her, saying nothing. Colleen stared back. No way was she going to tell him about Jesse. Wild horses couldn't have dragged it out of her.

"I met someone," Colleen said.

Mark grinned. "I knew it! Tell Uncle Marky all about it. Is he a strong, powerful businessman with a penchant for rooms painted like cherries?"

"Um, no." Colleen shivered as she thought of how Jesse had knelt for her, then got herself under control. She gave Mark a stern look. "And you're not my uncle."

"Doctor? Lawyer?"

"No!" She shook her head, trying not to laugh because that would only encourage him, and dammit, Mark could be totally out of line and completely nuts, but he was damned good at getting to the heart of things.

"He's a professor. You always did like the smarty-pants types."

"No." She paused, then with a sigh, owned up. "He's a bartender."

Mark steepled his fingertips below his chin. "Ah. That's quite a departure for you."

"Don't you judge him for being a bartender!"

"Are you sure *you're* not judging him for being a bartender?" Colleen's mouth closed with an audible snap. Mark grinned again. He shook a finger at her. "Ah, ah, ah. It's not what a man does. It's who he is that matters."

"I don't know who he is. Just that he's a bartender. And he's younger. And if you call me a cougar, I swear I will jump across that desk and throttle you with your own tie."

Mark frowned. "So violent."

Colleen sniffed and sipped her terrible coffee.

"I'd never call you a cougar. That's entirely too predatory. And something tells me this younger guy, this bartender, pursued you."

Heat flooded her at the memory of it. She put her mug on the desk and linked her fingers together. "It was mutual."

"He made you feel something." Mark shook a finger again. "I can tell."

"It was nothing. There was nothing, it was just…a weekend thing, we were snowed in. I was upset about Steve, and I went to the bar, and it was just… It just happened. That's all. And then a few times after that."

"And you're still seeing him?"

"Oh. No."

It was all over now. She'd let herself get too close too fast. She'd let herself miss Jesse and want him. And he'd known it, too, because she'd admitted it.

"You needed me," Jesse had said.

And it had been true.

"You're stupid," Mark said flatly. "This guy blew your skirt up in a major way."

"I didn't say that!"

"You didn't have to. I've known you for what, fifteen years now? And in all that time, I've never heard you so much as whisper the mention of another man's name besides that asshole ex-husband." Mark shrugged and recrossed his feet. "So this guy must've done something right."

Jesse had done everything right, that was the problem.

"Can I get back to work now?"

"Not until you tell me what it was about this guy that got you so flustered." Mark flicked a glance toward the office door. "Then you can go make me more money."

Colleen sighed and rubbed gently at the spot between her eyes for a second, unwilling to put into words what she'd been avoiding thinking about since leaving Jesse's apartment. Mark wouldn't let it go. And there was something about confession being good for the soul, right?

"He was really accommodating. Really sweet. And he seemed to know how to... He liked to... I mean, he was okay with me being... Shit."

Mark's feet hit the floor with a thump and he leaned forward, face serious. "Spill it."

"Maybe Steve's right, that's all." Colleen swallowed bitterness at the admission.

"About you needing to control everything?"

It burned that Mark knew that, but she nodded.

He snorted derision. "The guy who's trying to force you into putting up tacky copper schools of fish in every room of your condo is still trying to tell you that you're the one with control issues?"

"What were you doing, listening to my conversation?" Colleen fought for outrage but narrowly missed it.

"The whole office could hear you. The walls in here are shit." Mark shook his head, mock sorrow all over his face that faded into a stern look. "Listen up. All Steve knows is how to be bitter, bitter and more bitter because you didn't want spend the rest of your life catering to his every whim."

"He's not wrong about me, Mark. I do like things a certain way. I do like to be in charge."

"And?" Mark demanded, and waited for her to answer. When she didn't, he sneered. "Any man who can't deal with a strong, capable woman who knows her own mind doesn't deserve her. The truth is, and listen to your Uncle Marky on this one, Steve was too intimidated by you. He was scared of you. And that's his problem, not yours. If this bartender gave you a good time, where's the harm?"

"I liked being with him."

"That's the way it works, Colleen. You meet someone. You hit it off. You like them—"

She shook her head. "He did things for me, Mark."

"I assumed so."

She made a face at his lecherous expression. "No. I mean, other things. He fixed my fireplace and shoveled out my car. I started to like him. And when we didn't talk, I missed him. And I didn't want to get used to him being there, to needing him."

There is was, out in the open, sounding so stupid she couldn't believe she'd admitted it. She pressed her lips together, thinking of all the times Steve had done or said things to convince her she wasn't capable of taking care of herself. Of how he'd done worse things than that to keep her dependent on him. Needing him.

"I didn't want to be what Steve said I was."

Mark got up then and came around to sit on the edge of the desk in front of her. "Colleen, you could never be what Steve said you are. Not ever."

Her shoulders slumped. She didn't want to cry in Mark's office, though she'd certainly had more than a few breakdowns in there. Not for a couple years, though. She didn't want to backslide. When her boss put a hand on her shoulder, squeezing gently, Colleen let out a long, slow sigh.

"Look," Mark said. "My brother is a giant dick of the highest order. He gets it from our father, who was the king of Megadick Mountain. Some people, Steve included, I'm sure, think his behavior is excusable because of how we were raised, but the truth is, you either let that shit weigh you down forever, or you get over it and make something of your life that's not broken because of what your parents did to you. My brother is a douche with control issues and a drinking problem, and he treated you terribly, and I'm sorry. But the longer you let him make you feel like shit about who you are because he feels that way about himself, the longer you have to deal with feeling like shit. Get out there and get what you want, Colleen."

She gave him a small, hard smile. "Is that your version of a pep talk?"

"So I won't win any awards for motivational speaking." Mark shrugged and went back to his chair. "But you know I'm right."

She stared at him for half a minute before nodding. "Yeah. I know you're right."

"So tell him that. Apologize if you have to, eat crow. Get

on your knees and beg him for another chance." Mark narrowed his eyes, looking her over. "Or make him get on his, if that's your flavor. But whatever you do, don't let him walk out of your life."

"He didn't walk out. I threw him out." The admission rasped on her tongue, the truth barbed.

Mark shrugged. "Then admit you were stupid and go after him. What's the worst that could happen?"

"I could want him and need him, and he could let me down." Saying it out loud sounded so dumb she had to laugh. "But I already want him."

"So, let yourself need him, too."

Colleen sighed. "I'm not very good at letting go."

Mark leaned forward on the desk. "Take your Uncle Marky's advice, Colleen. Get better at it."

CHAPTER ELEVEN

The paperwork had all been put into place. The amount of the loan that she'd thought so daunting was the price of freedom, and you couldn't put a price on that, could you? All of it had taken only two weeks to put together. Colleen tapped the papers neatly together and slipped them into the folder, capped her fountain pen and slipped it into the soft felt case, then tucked it into her purse. She straightened, smoothing her skirt and brushing off her blouse, then patted her hair into place.

She was ready to kick some ass.

"You did something different with your hair," Steve said when she sat down at the table. "I liked it better the other way."

Colleen had never liked this restaurant, which was why she'd agreed to come here. At least nothing that happened today could ruin it for her. "I'm sure you did."

"You changed the color? What?"

"I haven't done anything to it, Steve. That's why it's different. I haven't done anything to it." No cut, perm, color, highlights, nothing. Colleen took a calming breath. This wasn't about her hair. She slid the folder across the table to him. "Let's get this over with."

"Over with? C'mon, something to eat. The pasta here's great. Remember?" Steve gave her what she was sure was meant to be a winning grin, but it left her unmoved. And the glint in his eyes that used to make her anxious left her just as unconcerned.

She'd changed. She pushed the folder with her fingertips. "I don't care for anything, thank you. I'd like to go over this stuff with you and get out of here. I've got things to do."

Steve sat and stared at her, not touching the folder. In fact, he'd recoiled from it, as though it were covered in slime. He took a long drink from his glass of ice water.

"What is this?"

"I'd like to buy you out of the beach property." Colleen folded her hands in her lap. "I've pulled together all the financials on it and I've prepared an offer that I think is more than fair."

"You can't afford to buy me out. You need me to be able to afford it." He said it so smugly, so arrogantly, that if it weren't for the flash of genuine fear in his eyes, Colleen would've hated him.

As it was, for the first time in dealing with him, instead of anger or fear, Colleen felt some pity for Steve. "I can, actually. You don't have to accept my offer, certainly, but if you don't, you're going to have to buy me out. I'm willing to take the same agreement."

"You can't give up the condo. You love the beach too much."

If he bought her out, she could buy another condo, or even a cute bungalow. "I do love the beach, Steve, but I don't love sharing it with you. And I don't want to do it any longer. You've made every part of owning this property an utter hell. Kind of like our marriage."

His jaw dropped. Colleen was shocked she'd said it, too, but once the words were out, it was as though each of them had been a brick stacked up on her shoulders and speaking them aloud had knocked them all to the ground. Her hands twisted, fingers tangling in her lap.

"Let me buy you out," she said. "You don't want that condo, not really. You only kept it as a way to control me."

His reaction showed her that she'd made a point. A really sharp one, and it had poked him someplace tender. He still didn't open the folder.

"You can't afford it," he repeated, with less assurance. "You…you need me."

Colleen smiled. "I assure you, I can. And I don't. But that's really not your business, is it?"

"I don't want to see you get yourself in trouble, that's all."

"I'm not your problem anymore, Steve."

They stared at each other across the table, and in that moment, it wasn't difficult for her to remember that once upon a time, a long time ago, she'd looked at this man with love in her eyes. A lot had come between them since then. She would never love him again. But she didn't have to let what had happened between them define her any longer.

Angrily, he flipped open the folder and thumbed through the pages. His shoulders slumped as he went over everything she'd put together. The layout of the financials, the division of items in the property, the amount she was prepared to offer up front and the timetable for the two additional lump sum payments she'd planned for.

"You've done a lot of work on this."

She nodded. Steve sighed and flipped through more pages. There wasn't much else to see. She'd made all of it as straightforward as possible. He could keep most of the furnishings and decorative items, and she'd pay him slightly over half of what they still owed on the property. Still, she wouldn't have put it past him to argue with her about it. Or even flat out refuse.

"I never liked that place. Everything's damp all the time. And it's cheap, shoddy construction. And the town is shit. If I want a vacation place, I'm going to get one in the Caribbean."

"You'll be able to do whatever you want," Colleen said.

Steve frowned. "I don't have a pen."

"I have one."

She passed him one she had ready from her purse. Not the fountain pen, but a cheap stick pen that, sure enough, he tucked into his pocket when he'd finished. She didn't even think he did it on purpose, it was just Steve's habit to consider everything he touched to be his. He shoved the folder back toward her.

It was her turn not to touch it. It had been a huge step for her, the last step toward completely breaking free of Steve and their marriage. The money situation was definitely nerve-racking, even though she'd run the numbers a couple dozen times and knew she could do it.

She could do all of this.

"Thanks," she told him sincerely. "This means a lot to me. Thank you."

"Don't come crying to me when you're defaulting on your loan and can't pay the mortgage on that hipster row house you bought. I told you not to," Steve added. "Fell's Point isn't any place for anyone to really *live*."

Colleen smiled. "I love it there."

"Well. It's just...fine." Steve drained his glass of ice water. "You want to drink to it?"

It was a test to see if she'd encourage him. So he could blame her for falling off the wagon. "No, thanks."

"Still uptight, huh?" His grin, all teeth, had no humor in it.

But instead of being stung, Colleen only smiled a little wider. She took the folder and double-checked that all the signatures were where they belonged, then stood and tucked the folder under her arm. She didn't offer her hand. He wouldn't have taken it, anyway.

"Good luck, Steve. Take care."

He called after her, as she knew he would. Loud, belligerent, not caring that he turned heads. Convinced he was charming enough that everyone was chuckling along with him instead of shaking their heads in disapproval. But though he shouted her name a few times, increasingly louder and more strident, Colleen didn't turn around.

Another Thursday night, but Jesse didn't bother looking up to see if Colleen was going to walk through the Angel's door. She wasn't going to. And even if she did come into the bar to sit at that same stool and not drink that same glass of whiskey, why should it matter to him? She'd made it clear enough that she wasn't interested in anything to do with him.

That sucked.

He hadn't known her long enough to feel this disappointed. It was stupid. And lame. And dammit, he couldn't stop thinking about her.

He spent an hour in the basement, cataloging boxes of sugar packets and bottles of mustard and cartons of napkins. By the time he came upstairs, he'd managed to calm himself a little, at least enough so that when the bell jingled again, he didn't want to jump over the bar and pummel the crap out of the person who wasn't Colleen.

It was, to both Jesse and John's surprise, The Fallen Angel's owner. Rick Benjamin hardly ever came into the bar himself. Now he stamped snow off his boots and off the shoulders of his heavy winter coat.

"We're closing," he said to John. To the customers gathered around the tables and sitting at the bar, he announced, "Listen, folks, the weather report says that instead of another inch or so, we're looking at a possible six to ten, along with freezing rain. I got an update from the power company that outages are likely. My advice to all of you is to head home and stay safe and warm."

"Again?" John said. "Who pissed off Mother Nature?"

Jesse was already gathering up the few empty glasses and putting them in the plastic bin to take back to the kitchen. At Rick's warning, everyone in the bar got up and started putting on their coats.

"Scattered like the wind," John said. "Look at them go."

Rick snorted with laughter and looked at Jesse. "Leave that stuff. It's bad out there and getting worse. I'm closing up tonight and for tomorrow, too, just to be safe. I'll let everyone know how Saturday's looking. But get out of here."

As Jesse grabbed his own coat, his phone buzzed. Laila's school, announcing another day closed. He texted Diane to make sure she and the kid were okay, then headed to his car. Rick had been right. It would've been smart for him to head straight home and get out of the storm, but he remembered there was nothing in the fridge but some ready-to-expire yogurt and some limp celery. Jesse frowned as he pulled into the grocery store parking lot. Better stock up, he thought, before he was snowed in—sadly, by himself this time.

Spring couldn't get here fast enough, Colleen thought as she snagged one of the last carts at the grocery store and managed to avoid being run over by a woman who'd filled her buggy with bulk packages of toilet paper. The small grocery store didn't carry a lot of stock as it was, but even so the aisles were incredibly picked over. She was able to grab some salad and a bag of apples, as well as some canned spaghetti and ravioli. Also some sardines, because what the hell, if she was going to prepare for what looked to be the Snowpocalypse, she might as well make sure she had a wide variety of things on which she could survive. Besides, she didn't have to fight anyone for the sardines. She'd have shoved someone for one of those packages of Oreos, though.

"Oh," she said, startled. "Hi."

Jesse turned, the last package of cookies in his hand. He looked good. Beard a little scruffy, hair rumpled where it showed beneath the navy stocking cap. He didn't smile when he saw her, and that broke her heart a little.

"You've got my favorite," she told him.

He didn't look at the cookies. Just at her. "Yeah?"

"Yeah. Oreos. My favorite. Think we could snag some milk to go with them? The shelves are getting picked pretty bare." She kept her voice light. Casual. But she made sure to keep eye contact.

Jesse stepped to one side to show her the cart his body had been hiding before. In it, a gallon jug of milk, a few bags of potato chips, some paper plates and napkins. He had a box of white utility candles, too. He didn't say anything. Just let her look.

"In case the power goes out?" she asked, pointing at the disposables.

He nodded.

"Milk and cookies by candlelight. Could be romantic."

His mouth twitched the tiniest amount. She couldn't blame him for keeping his smile tethered down. She couldn't blame

113

herself for trying to tease one out of him anyway. She held up her sardines without saying anything, just a wiggle of her brows she meant to be deliberately strange and suggestive.

Jesse gave in. He laughed, she laughed with him and suddenly everything seemed as though it might actually be okay. Colleen took a chance and stepped closer. He didn't move away.

"I missed you," Jesse blurted out and looked instantly as though he regretted it.

Her heart broke more than a little this time. She moved near enough to touch his face. The way he closed his eyes at her touch told her everything she needed to know. Everything she'd been hoping was true.

"I missed you, too." Then she kissed him. Right there in the middle of the store, oblivious to anyone who might be watching, not giving a damn if she was making a mistake. She kissed him, kissed him, kissed him.

Jesse kissed her back. His arms went around her, squeezing hard enough to crackle the cookie package. She didn't care. All that mattered was that he was holding her. That she had a chance to make things okay, if she was willing to take it. It might not work out. She might have to eat crow, like Mark said. And even then it might be too late.

But she had to try.

"Come home with me," Colleen said against his mouth. "Let's get snowed in together."

Jesse drew back enough to look into her eyes. She wouldn't have been surprised if she'd seen hesitation there, wouldn't have blamed him for saying no. But, as with everything else he'd ever done, Jesse didn't disappoint her.

"Yes," he said. "Let's go."

★ ★ ★ ★ ★

DEDICATION

To Mrs. Colvin, my freshman high school English teacher,
who introduced me to Romeo, Juliet, Paris, The Nurse
and (of course) the one and only Mercutio.

Shakespeare and I have been star-crossed lovers ever since...

ABOUT THE AUTHOR

Tiffany Reisz is an award-winning and internationally
bestselling author of The Original Sinners series (Harlequin MIRA).
When she's not writing scandalous tales about naughty priests and
quirky dominatrices, she's doing sordid things to Shakespeare plays.
She lives in Lexington, Kentucky, with her fiancé and two weird cats.
Contact her at tiffany@tiffanyreisz.com if you dare.

Also by Tiffany Reisz

Cosmo Red-Hot Reads from Harlequin
MISBEHAVING

The Original Sinners Series
THE MISTRESS
THE PRINCE
THE ANGEL
THE SIREN

Novellas
THE MISTRESS DIARIES
THE GIFT (originally published as SEVEN DAY LOAN)
SUBMIT TO DESIRE
IMMERSED IN PLEASURE

Dear Reader,

I hope you enjoyed *Misbehaving*, my first Cosmo Red-Hot Reads from Harlequin story. Now I'm back with *Seize the Night*, a new sexy Shakespeare retelling for your reading pleasure.

When Harlequin asked me for a second Cosmo Red-Hot Reads from Harlequin story, I went for a long bike ride to think about what I should write. Since *Misbehaving* was a modern erotic update of the comedy *Much Ado About Nothing*, maybe I'd try my hand at retelling a tragedy. There's no more famous romance in the history of English literature than the one between Romeo and Juliet. I live in Lexington, Kentucky, also known as the "Horse Capital of the World," and as I rode, I saw horses everywhere. There's lots of drama in horse racing, lots of money, beauty and romance, too. Could I update *Romeo and Juliet* to fit into this world? Of course I could! I took out the death, added a lot of sex, set it among two rival horse-racing families, threw in a happy ending and turned Mercutio's infamous line "A plague on both your houses" into my Merrick's "A plague on both your horses!"

What can I say? I was an English major. This is how I put my degree to use.

Friends, Romans, Harlequin readers, lend me your eyes. I give you the story of Remi O. Montgomery, manager of Arden Farms, and her star-crossed love affair with Julien Brite of Capital Hills Farms.

Happy reading!

Tiffany Reisz

PS Fans of my Original Sinners series will catch a few inside jokes. Sorry Wesley couldn't come to the party. He was busy up north with a certain green-eyed Damn Yankee of our acquaintance.

SEIZE THE NIGHT

by
Tiffany Reisz

CHAPTER ONE

The Winner's Circle

The boy in blue started the fight but the boy in red finished it. Swearing turned to yelling, which led to shoving and punching within seconds. Remi fished her phone out of her messenger bag, called the security office, and two minutes later the fight was over. Both young men—college kids by the looks of them—were being escorted away. Too much alcohol and testosterone. Too little good sense.

Remi felt the needle prick of her conscience. She couldn't judge them, tempting as it was. She'd been that age not too long ago, and she remembered being that stupid. Remembered it all too well.

Still, it made no sense to her. Two guys in opposing jerseys fighting at a football game would hardly have been a surprise. Or even a baseball or a basketball game. But this was Verona Downs. When did college boys start getting into fistfights over racehorses? Bizarre. *Bizarre* was the only word for it.

Bizarre was also the only word for the man who entered the grandstand and strode toward Remi's seat. He wore all black, as usual. His slacks, his button-down shirt (untucked, of course), leather bracelets on both wrists, shoes, socks and underwear (if he did, in fact, wear underwear), and sunglasses were all black. Under the black sunglasses lurked intelligent blue eyes usually narrowed in suspicion or derision. Most of the women in the stands watched his progress. She didn't blame them. He was in his mid-thirties, annoyingly handsome and wasn't smiling. He had an "I can't wait to rock your world in bed and then make you regret you ever met me" look about him. Women fell for that look often. She hadn't. She had zero desire to sleep with him. He was Merrick Feingold. Unlike the women who were lusting at him at this moment, Remi had met him.

"Why, pray tell, am I sitting among the plebeians?" Merrick asked as he took his seat next to her. They must have made an odd pair—him in his mysterious all-black attire and she in faded jeans, a tailored plaid shirt and cowboy boots. He looked like a rock star while she tended toward stable girl.

"This is not ancient Rome, and these are not plebeians. These are people just like us," Remi said as she made a notation in her leather journal. "And you're sitting here because your boss wants your sunshiny self sitting right next to her."

"We have that nice Arden Farms private box right over there," Merrick said, pointing at the clubhouse balcony section where all the horse owners had private air-conditioned boxes. "This 'man of the people' routine of yours is infringing on my creature comforts."

"This is not a 'man of the people' routine," Remi said. "First of all, I *am* the people, not *of* the people. *We* are people. Second, I am not a man."

"Prove it," Merrick said.

"Do I look like a man to you?"

"No. You look like a hot blonde with spectacular tits,

which are probably fake, since for all I know, you might be a man."

"I'm not sleeping with you. I'm your employer. You are my assistant."

"Until I see you naked I won't know if you're actually a man or a woman. It's like Schrödinger's Pussy."

"You just used quantum physics to hit on me. I'm almost impressed."

"Impressed enough to sleep with me?" Merrick asked.

"No."

Merrick shrugged. He seemed philosophical about her refusal and not the least disappointed. For all his quantum flirting, Merrick's interest in her was merely mechanical. And she had no interest in him at all. She was twenty-six and he was thirty-six. To her Merrick was like an older brother. An older brother she paid to do whatever she told him to do. The best sort of older brother. The type she could fire.

Remi's cell phone buzzed in her bag. She dug it out and looked at the name. Now she remembered why she'd hired Merrick.

"Ugh. Help. It's Brian Roseland." Remi handed the phone to Merrick.

"You want me to do the thing?" he asked.

"Please and thank you."

"Yell-o?" Merrick said, taking the call for her. "No, Remi's not here right now. She's on a date."

Remi covered her mouth to stifle a laugh. Her? On a date on a Thursday afternoon? Good thing Merrick was a better liar than she was.

"She's been gone all week, Mr. Roseland," Merrick said. "It's that kind of date. One with traveling and exotic locations and them sticking body parts into each other."

Remi grabbed for the phone. Merrick jerked it away.

"But I'll tell her you called once she gets back from her weeklong exotic-locale sex date." Merrick tugged her ponytail to annoy her. It worked.

Then he ended the call and handed her the phone.

"I told Roseland you were on an exotic-locale weeklong sex date," Merrick said.

"Yes, I heard that part. Did you have to go into that much detail?" she demanded.

"Look, Boss," Merrick said, "either learn how to lie to people or leave me alone when you make me do your lying for you."

"Fine. Thank you for getting rid of him. Third time he's called me this week," she said. "Maybe if he thinks I'm on a date he'll finally get the hint that it's completely over."

Remi dropped her phone back in her bag just as the post parade began. The outriders trotted alongside the jockeys astride their racehorses. Her own Arden Farms jockey, Mike Alvarez, in his red-and-white silks, threw a smile at the crowd as he and their three-year-old filly Shenanigans passed the grandstand.

"Boss, are you ever going to tell me why you dumped Roseland?" Merrick asked, as she made a note in her journal.

"Never."

"Please? I'll whimper. Don't make me whimper." He whimpered.

"Do you really care?" she asked. "Or is this just perverse curiosity about my sex life?"

"I care desperately in a perversely curious-about-your-sex-life way," Merrick said. "You never tell me anything about your personal life. You don't hit on me. You ignore me when I hit on you. You keep our work relationship professional no matter how hard I try to make it unprofessional. It's like you have integrity or something, and quite frankly, I'm sick of it."

Remi closed her journal.

"If I tell you, will you shut up for two whole minutes during the race?"

"Two minutes? I can do that. Talk," Merrick ordered.

"When I started dating the handsome Mr. Roseland, I thought he was a really nice guy," she began.

"No wonder you dumped him," Merrick said. She glowered at him. He whimpered in response.

"I happen to like nice guys," she said, and a face from her past flashed in front of her eyes. A young, handsome, smiling face—near-black eyes, dark red hair, a smile both sweet and striking. She kicked the memory out of her mind—a futile gesture. She knew it would only gallop back in her brain. "In fact, I love nice guys. It just turned out Brian wasn't a nice guy."

Merrick pushed his sunglasses up on top of his head and stared at her.

"If he hurt you, you tell me right now, Remi," he said. He only called her Remi in his rare moods of deadly seriousness. He'd probably called her by her first name all of twice in two years. The rest of the time she was just "Boss." "If he got rough with you I will get rough with him. That prick can watch the horses race from his boxed seats in Hell."

She shook her head.

"No, he didn't hurt me," she said, touched by Merrick's devotion. They harassed and insulted each other, but at the heart of their working relationship was a solid core of respect and loyalty. And near-constant exasperation on her part. "I promise. I'd kick his ass if he tried. It was just that... So three months ago, Brian and I were...you know..."

"Twerking?"

"Fucking. And the condom broke. I'm on birth control, but I still panicked. Abject white-knuckle panic."

"Is Roseland a heroin addict?"

"Clean as a whistle and so am I. But even the thought of having a baby with Brian terrified me. I couldn't imagine spending Christmas with him, much less marrying him and having kids. It was a horrible thought. So we broke up."

She spoke matter-of-factly, but the break-up had been anything but matter-of-fact. Brian had been furious and accusatory, demanding to know if she was cheating on him. He'd been so bitterly angry he'd scared her, and from that moment on, she had refused to see him or speak to him. His ensuing profanity-laden tantrum had proven that her instincts to dump him had been dead-on.

"That's the whole story?" Merrick asked, sounding skeptical.

"That's it. I broke up with him. He threw a hissy fit about it. The end."

"Well, you are *easily* the second or third most beautiful woman in north-central Kentucky."

"Thank you for that regionally specific compliment," she said. "Now shut up. It's post time."

Merrick went silent as all six horses were slotted into the starting gate. Any second now the bell would ring and the horses would burst from the gates. It was just an ordinary race on a Thursday afternoon at Verona Downs. Not even a stakes race. And yet it looked like the Kentucky Derby for all the press there and the grandstand packed with fans. At least fifty people had brought homemade signs that bore the words, I Call Shenanigans! Did these people not realize that horses, unlike football or baseball players, could not read?

Remi held her breath.

The bell rang, and the horses exploded down the track in a furor of pounding hooves and streaming colors. The crowd around them cheered and clapped and roared. She and Merrick watched the race in silence.

After two minutes and a mile and a half had passed, Shenanigans of Arden Farms was declared the unofficial winner. Remi should have been happy that their champion filly had won the race. A nice purse, a sweet victory, another trophy in the trophy room...

"You don't look happy, Bubbalah," Merrick said and put two fingers on either side of her face, forcing her lips into a smile. She gave him the most glaring of death glares. "Your little pony won her race. Smile like you mean it."

The outrider led Mike and Shenanigans on a victory lap.

"Let's go," she said.

"Thank God," Merrick said, as they stood up. "I'm starting to sweat. It's October. I don't let myself sweat in October."

She grabbed her things, and Merrick let her out into the aisle. He followed behind her as she strode to the rails.

"Have you noticed anything weird here lately?" she asked him.

"Yes. Definitely. What the hell does that woman have on top of her head? A sailboat?" He pointed at a lady walking past their section. "Ahoy there!" he shouted at the woman in the white hat with the voluminous veil. "No one can see over your damn schooner! Full steam ahead!"

"Merrick, please behave yourself."

"Why? You're in the cheap seats. Nobody knows that YOU'RE REMI MONTGOMERY AND YOUR FAMILY OWNS SHENANIGANS, THE WINNING HORSE." Merrick spoke so loudly everyone in a twenty-yard radius heard him. Of course they did.

"And you wonder why I won't ever sleep with you," she whispered to him.

"AND YOU AND I AREN'T SLEEPING TO-

GETHER," Merrick said, still in his obnoxious booming voice. Everyone in the grandstands stared at them as they walked down to the viewing area in front of the track.

"Remind me why I hired you again." Remi slid her bag over her shoulder as they headed to the clubhouse.

"Because you wanted someone outside the racing indus-try who didn't give a fuck about horse racing to be your as-sistant. Also I'm brilliant *and* the sexiest man alive."

"Two out of three ain't bad. Come here, I want to show you something," she said, pausing at the track to watch the jockey weigh-in. The results of the race wouldn't be official until the jockeys were weighed.

"Finally. But let's find a stall so we can have some privacy for our first time. I want it to be as awkward and uncom-fortable as possible for the both of us."

She opened her bag and handed him a magazine.

"Wow," Merrick said, a word she'd never heard pass his lips before. Merrick was not easily impressed. "You don't see horses on the cover of *Sports Illustrated* very often. Then again, I only 'read' the swimsuit issue."

Remi stood next to him as they stared at the cover—She-nanigans, her family's chestnut filly, and Hijinks, the Capital Hills colt, barreled down the center of the Verona Downs track toward the camera. The picture had been snapped in the final stretch of the Lexington Stakes—a glorious action shot of two beautiful beasts running their guts out.

"Look at that headline. The New Civil War—Hijinks Ver-sus Shenanigans in the Horse Racing Rivalry of the Cen-tury," Remi read aloud, trying not to roll her eyes at the hyperbole. "They called us the Hatfields and McCoys of horse racing."

"That'll sell some T-shirts." Merrick handed her the mag-azine.

"This article is ridiculous," Remi said, flipping through the pages. "It's all about the vicious rivalry between Arden Farms and Capital Hills—two of the oldest Kentucky horse farms. Everyone's picking a side—Team Shenanigans versus Team Hijinks."

"I'm still Team Edward."

"I saw a fight today right by the rails. It was between two guys, one wearing an Arden shirt, the other guy in a Capital Hills shirt. After this feature, the entire racing world will be betting on Shenanigans and Hijinks. They're even selling Hijinks and Shenanigans stuffed animals.."

"Now that's just sick."

"Tell me about it. These horses are turning into money trees."

"You say that like it's a bad thing. Shenanigans is your family's horse," he reminded her. "More notoriety, better attendance, better press, more money, more money for me, your faithful assistant who deserves a raise. Should I write this down for you?"

"Write this down for me," she said, handing Merrick a pen and her journal. "One hundred million and two hundred million. Got it?"

He held up the page where he'd written the figures. "So?"

"One hundred million is how much money is bet on the Kentucky Derby. Two hundred million is how much is bet on the Breeders' Cup."

"And I wrote them down why?"

Remi shook her head and turned to the Winner's Circle. Her mother and father stood next to Shenanigans while the assembled press frantically took pictures.

"You wrote them down because I want you to see how much money there is in horse racing."

"Fine. I'll buy a goddamn pony."

"I wouldn't trust you with a goldfish, Merrick. That's not my point," Remi said.

"What's your point then?"

She exhaled hard and shook her head. She'd been dreading this question, because she'd been dreading the answer to it. Still, Merrick was the one person in her life she trusted right now, so she thought she might as well tell him.

"My parents bought a new farm a couple months ago," she said. "Satellite Farm—five hundred acres."

"So?"

"They paid cash for it. Ten million dollars. We shouldn't have had ten million dollars in cash lying around."

"And?"

"I don't know," she admitted. "But we shouldn't have that much money lying around. Capital Hills seems to have had a windfall, too. The auctions were this week—they dropped ten million the first three days."

"Damn."

"That's kind of a coincidence, isn't it? They suddenly have ten million dollars? We suddenly have ten million dollars?"

"A slightly suspicious coincidence," Merrick said, narrowing his eyes at her parents.

"That's what I was thinking. Three months ago Dad changed the passwords on the bank accounts. I can't see how much money we have anymore. I told him a while ago to hire a new accountant, and that was his excuse—new guy, new passwords. Don't worry my pretty little head about it."

"Your pretty little head looks worried."

"Rivalries always make for money and headlines. But, Merrick, I don't know. Something doesn't smell right about this. And trust me, my family and the Capital Hills family aren't in anything together. They hate each other."

"I've noticed that."

"But still, I think someone at Arden and someone at Capital Hill might be stoking this rivalry in the press for a reason."

"What reason?" Merrick asked. "Money?"

"Is there any other reason?" Remi asked, feeling sick to her stomach even saying that much. "Tyson Balt was at our house last night."

"He owns Verona Downs, right? VD for short? He really should have rethought that name. What about him?"

"Balt's been promoting the hell out of the Verona Downs Stakes race. Shenanigans and Hijinks are the two favorites already."

"You think your family is getting the money from Balt?"

"Something's not right" was all she would say.

Merrick pursed his lips and whistled.

"I don't have the evidence yet. It's only a hunch," Remi said.

"You really want to dig this hole? You might end up falling into it, Boss."

"I know," she said, her stomach tightening. "But if my hunch is right, there's a fraud being perpetuated here at Verona. I can't look the other way even if my own family is involved. This farm has been my life for twenty-six years. I'm not going to let them fuck it up."

"We should talk to someone at Capital Hills. What's their name? The Brites?" Merrick asked.

Remi swallowed. Heat rushed to her face.

"Yes," she said, her voice neutral. "The Capital Hills farm has been in the Brite family for 150 years."

"The parents are out since they're probably in on this, whatever it is," Merrick said. "And we can't talk to the daughters. I banged two out of three of them and didn't call after."

"Wait. When did that happen?"

"What was that thing with the big hats you dragged me to in May?"

"The Kentucky Derby?"

"That."

"You had a threesome with two of the three Brite daughters at the Kentucky Derby?"

"You say that like it's a bad thing."

"This is why I can't take you anywhere. Okay, so the sisters are out."

"Two out of three are. Anyone else?" Merrick asked. "A trainer maybe? Maybe we can find a stable boy you can bat your tits and flash your eyelashes at."

"I doubt a groom would know anything."

"A higher-up, then? A secretary?"

Remi shifted uncomfortably as her parents smiled for the dozens of cameras in the Winner's Circle. Even Shenanigans seemed to be smiling.

"Well…I guess we can talk to Julien Brite," Remi said and a tiny tremor passed through her body as his name passed her lips.

"Which one's Julien?"

"Julien is the son. He's the youngest in the family."

"Never heard of him," Merrick said.

"He's not in the business," Remi said. "Not sure why. I don't even know where he lives now."

"You know him?"

"Sort of."

Merrick narrowed his eyes at her. "You sort of know him? Can you trust him?"

"He's the only member of the Brite family who doesn't hate me. I think."

"He sounds like our guy, then. You want to find him and go talk to him about this stupid rivalry?"

"Oh, he already knows about the rivalry," Remi said with a heavy sigh. "But yes, he's probably the only one in the Brite family we can talk to."

"I'll find his number," Merrick said. "We can call him."

"No calls," she said, making the decision at once. "On the off chance he does hate me, let's not give him a reason to hang up on us."

Remi stepped away from the rails and headed toward the clubhouse.

"So we show up on his doorstep and beg for help?"

"Can you find his doorstep for me? I'll do the begging."

"On it, Boss. But if Julien isn't involved in the business, how do you know he knows anything about the rivalry?" Merrick asked. The crowd ahead parted for them. The people in the grandstand might not have known who she and Merrick were, but the clubhouse crowd certainly did. Tyson Balt, the owner of Verona Downs, eyed her warily. The feeling was entirely mutual. And up in the boxes she saw Mr. and Mrs. Brite giving an interview to a reporter as a camera recorded their every word. She glanced up at them. They glared down at her with unmistakable loathing.

"Because," Remi sighed, "four years ago, Julien and I accidentally started it."

CHAPTER TWO

Vive La France

On Friday morning, Remi and Merrick boarded an airplane. Halfway through the flight Remi realized she'd been digging her hand into Merrick's knee for the past two hours. Flying didn't scare her. She'd spent too many years on the back of high-jumping horses to be afraid of a little altitude. But even after four hours of smooth sailing, Remi remained a rapidly fraying knot of tension.

"Boss? You okay?" Merrick asked as he signaled the flight attendant for another drink. He was having way too much fun in first class, much more fun than she was. "I mean, I don't mind that you're squeezing my knee so hard I can't feel my calf, but there are other body parts I could direct your attention to, if you're interested."

"Steady as she goes." Remi took the vodka out of his hand and chugged it.

"Whoa, Nellie." Merrick grabbed it back. "We've got five hours left on this flight."

"Sorry," she said. "Take it. I'm fine."

"Yeah, you seem real fucking fine. What's wrong?"

"Nothing."

"How many times do I have to tell you that you're the world's worst liar?" Merrick asked. "You're stressed about seeing this Julien guy again. Yes?"

"A smidge," she said. "A skosh."

"Are you going to tell me why?"

She shook her head. "Not if you won't let me have your vodka."

He gave her the vodka. "Sip it and talk. You can't say something like 'Julien and I started this rivalry' and sashay off all dramatic-like without telling me the story."

"It's a humiliating story," Remi said.

"Miss?" Merrick addressed the passing flight attendant. "I'm going to need some popcorn."

"Merrick."

"Talk," he said. "And don't leave out any juicy details."

"I'm leaving out all the juicy details," she said. "You get the bare bones."

"Is there boning involved in the bare bones?"

"Near boning," she said, wincing. She took a steadying breath and focused her attention on the hum of the airplane engines. It comforted her, the sound of the engines reminding her she was thousands of miles and years away from the time and place of her greatest humiliation.

"Go on…" Merrick said.

"This was back when I was in college—just graduated, actually. Winter graduation. I'd come home for Christmas, and Mom and Dad dragged me to a big Christmas party at The Rails."

"That's that huge horse farm in Versailles, yes?"

"Yes, bigger than Capital Hills and Arden put together."

"Got it. So it's Christmas. It's a party. You're what? Twenty-one?" Merrick asked.

"Twenty-two," she said. "It was a formal party, so I had an excuse to buy an awesome dress. Jade strappy thing."

"Did it make your tits look good?"

"You could have seen them from space," she said.

"I approve. Continue, please."

"Anyway," she said and paused to sip Merrick's vodka. She hated the stuff but needed a little liquid fortification. "I was there about an hour before I saw this gorgeous guy. He was standing on the other side of the room talking to a big, hotshot Kentucky basketball player. So I assumed he was a University of Kentucky student, probably a freshman. He was drinking a glass of white wine, and he looked so handsome in his tuxedo. He had messy red hair. I couldn't take my eyes off him."

"Gross."

"Do you want to hear this story or not?"

"Tell."

"Julien was so beautiful that I had to chug a whole glass of wine just to work up the courage to go talk to him."

"And you did, and he was smart and funny and nice and all that boring shit women love?"

"All that and more," Remi said. "We walked through the house together. Gorgeous house. Every room decorated in a different Christmas theme. It was like something out of a fairy tale or a movie. I'd never seen anything like it, never felt anything like it. The night was perfect. Ever have a moment so perfect that you know you'll remember it the rest of your life while you're still living in the moment?"

"Never," Merrick said. "But it's a good dream. Too bad dreams lie."

"It felt like a dream, but it wasn't. This was real."

Remi closed her eyes and found herself once more in that house on that night. She and Julien stood by the fireplace mantel lined with a dozen yellow candles in antique brass candleholders. The room was filled with antique toys and a tree that soared all the way to the cathedral ceiling. The silver and gold stars on the tree reflected the dancing light from the fireplace. She'd never been the sort of girl who believed in love at first sight. And then she met Julien and that night, that one perfect night, she believed.

"This guy must have been special," Merrick said.

"I thought he could be." Remi knew she was the world's worst liar. Might as well tell the truth. "I didn't know how special he was, because he only told me his first name—Julien. We talked about everything and nothing. I don't even remember what we talked about except that he made me laugh and asked me questions like he wanted to know everything about me. Before I knew it, there we were, standing under the mistletoe."

"Best kiss ever?" Merrick asked.

"Best kiss ever," she agreed, remembering how Julien's lips had shivered lightly at the first gentle contact. The gentleness quickly turned to passion, and before she knew it, her arms were around his back and his mouth was on her neck, at her ear, at her throat. Every Christmas since then she'd thought of Julien. The lights, the tree, the scent of pine and candles brought the memories back. Maybe that's why she couldn't imagine spending Christmas with Brian Roseland. Christmas was already claimed by Julien and that one perfect night he'd been everything she'd wanted but never thought to ask for.

"I'm guessing the inevitable happened," Merrick said.

"We found an empty guest room. I thought I remembered locking the door behind us."

Merrick cringed. "I see where this is going…"

Remi nodded, her face flushing at the memory.

"We kissed for a long time. Julien seemed a little nervous,

and I didn't want to rush things since we'd just met. But then he unzipped the back of my dress and I unbuttoned his shirt...and his pants...and then."

"And then?"

"And then while things were happening, he said something weird and I stopped."

"Weird? What? Did he deny the Holocaust or something?"

"He said...'This feels better than I ever dreamt it would.'" Merrick cocked his head to the side.

"Ever *dreamt* it would? You mean he'd never had a girl do the thing on him before? I assume you were doing the thing."

"Oh, yeah. I was doing the thing. With gusto. And when he intimated that no woman had ever done the thing on him before, I sobered up and asked him how old he was."

"Oh fuck," Merrick said.

"Merrick, I was half naked on a bed with the virginal barely-seventeen-year-old son of one of the most powerful families in Thoroughbred racing."

"Oops."

"Two seconds after I told him we had to stop, the door opened. My dress was down, his jacket was off, his shirt was open, his pants were unzipped...and his mother saw it all."

Merrick's eyes went comically wide. Remi would have laughed but for the pain the memory still caused her.

"How bad was it?" Merrick asked. She appreciated that he seemed to understand the gravity of the situation instead of making Mrs. Robinson jokes.

"Bad. Julien's mom had had a little too much Christmas punch. It turned into a screaming match that everyone at the party heard."

"Oh, that's bad."

"Very bad. My parents showed up and started defending me. His parents called me every ugly name in the book. My father told Julien's father, 'Sir, control your wife.' And five minutes later, my father and his father were fighting. Like physically fighting. Dad gave Mr. Brite a black eye and Mr. Brite gave Dad a bloody nose. It's a miracle no one called the cops."

"Damn."

"The moms pulled the dads off each other, but that almost turned into a catfight until Mr. and Mrs. Railey showed up and calmed everyone down. Poor Julien was begging everyone to just shut up and leave us alone so he and I could talk. Instead his parents dragged him—literally dragged him away from me—and he's apologizing to me the entire time. 'I'm so sorry, Remi. I should have told you. I'm so sorry...'"

She could still hear his humiliated words ringing in her ears.

"And that started the feud?" Merrick asked.

"That was the beginning. My parents were furious at the Brites for making a scene and accusing me of seducing their baby boy. The Brites were furious at my parents because my parents blamed Julien for lying to me about his age. He didn't lie, for the record. I didn't ask him his age. Never occurred to me to ask until it was almost too late. And I just stood there in shock, saying nothing and feeling like I was going to puke and trying to get my dad not to kill his dad. I didn't get to talk to him, tell him I was sorry, tell him goodbye, even. It was awful."

"You didn't do anything illegal," Merrick said. "You were only twenty-two. And legal age in Kentucky is sixteen."

"Do I want to know why you have that legal factoid memorized?"

"Nope," he said. "So you never saw Julien again?"

"My parents forbade me from contacting Julien. I haven't seen him since that night. Not even at any of the races."

"Where did he go?"

She shrugged and tried to pretend that she had never looked for him and wondered that same question. Every race she'd looked for him.

"He disappeared. And that was that. Except his family still hasn't forgiven me for almost seducing their son, and my family still hasn't forgiven them for publicly humiliating me—us, really—at the party."

"Have you forgiven him?" Merrick asked.

Remi smiled. "Julien didn't do anything wrong. And while his mom was going batshit crazy on me, calling me every possible variation of *slut*, *whore* and *harlot*, he stood up to his parents and defended me."

"'Harlot'?"

"I believe the words 'blonde Jezebel' were also employed. Julien told her off. He told everyone off."

"Like a man. I approve."

"He's twenty-one now. I keep thinking I should…but it doesn't matter. It was a long time ago."

Merrick looked at her with searching serious eyes.

"You miss him," he said.

Remi didn't bother to deny it. "I had a perfect moment with him. You don't get many of those in your life."

"This was four years ago? You'd think your families would be over it after four fucking years."

"Judging by all the smack talk in the news, they aren't. In that *SI* interview, Mrs. Brite called us the 'white trash' farm."

"Classy."

"Dad called the Brites 'stuck-up snobs.' I'm really hoping Julien hasn't read that article."

"So what are you going to do when you see Julien again? Jump him?"

Remi laughed at the ludicrousness of the suggestion. She

hadn't seen him in four years, and the *only* reason she was seeing him now was to tell him their parents might be fixing races? Hardly cause for an erotic reunion.

"I'll do what I should have done years ago. I'll tell him I'm sorry."

After what felt like a year in the air, the plane landed. They checked into their hotel and Remi gave Merrick the night off. It was Saturday, after all. And all she wanted to do was sleep and recover from the flight. Merrick, however, had other plans.

"*Vive la France*, remember?" Merrick grabbed her by the upper arms and forced a kiss on each of her cheeks. "When in Paris, do as the Parisians do."

"What do the Parisians do?"

"I don't know," he admitted. "But I'm hoping it involves getting Parisian drunk and getting Parisian laid. Not necessarily in that Parisian order."

"I'm not drinking with you. Or any of the other options. Can't we go to bed? Not together?"

"We need to find this Brite boy of yours. My sources tell me he's a short Parisian cab ride away. Let's seize the Parisian day, Boss."

"It's night."

"Then let's seize the Parisian night."

"Are you going to put 'Parisian' in front of every noun until we leave?" Remi asked, as Merrick hailed a taxi.

"That would be a Parisian yes. I mean '*oui*.'"

Remi managed not to murder him during the ten minutes between their hotel and Julien's building.

The cab stopped in front of a nondescript three-story building. He paid the driver, which Remi thought was an unusually gallant gesture until she noticed Merrick was using her credit card. They stepped onto a side street off the Rue de Furstenberg.

Merrick half-escorted, half-dragged her to the door. "I think this is it. My sources tell me this is it," he said. "And by 'sources' I mean the Brite family housekeeper."

"Are you sure?" she asked. "I can't imagine any of the Brite family staying in someplace so normal. Well, normal for Paris, I mean."

"This has to be it. I paid ten whole dollars for his address."

"Your sources are cheap dates," Remi said. She rang the buzzer and dusted off her high school French.

"Bonjour?" came a woman's voice through the speaker. Woman? At Julien's house on a Saturday night? Remi hadn't planned for a girlfriend.

"Bonjour," Remi said, trying not to be bothered by the elegant voice. "Julien Brite, *s'il vous plaît?"*

"Your accent is terrible," the woman answered in English.

Remi laughed. "It's French by way of a Kentucky high school. Is Julien in?"

"He might be," the woman said in a clipped tone. She had something of an accent too but neither French nor Kentuckian. "Who are you?"

"I'm an old friend of his. I hope. My name is Remi Montgomery of Arden Farms. And—"

"Come up, please," the woman said before Remi could even finish her speech.

She looked at Merrick, who smiled at her in return.

"Look at you, Boss," he said. "You're famous."

The door buzzed, and they headed up the stairs to an apartment on the third floor.

Remi knocked and a woman opened the door. She looked about mid-thirties and was clearly of Indian descent, even though her clothes—a boatneck shirt, white scarf and stylish slacks—were pure Parisian chic. And she was beautiful beyond words. So beautiful even Merrick had gone speechless—something of a miracle.

"Oh, holy Parisian shit," Merrick finally said. So much for speechless.

"Excuse me?" the woman asked.

"You'll have to forgive Merrick here," Remi said, slapping Merrick on the back—hard. "You're beautiful, and he's a horrible person. Bad combination."

"Forgiven," she said. "Salena Kar. I work for Julien. You're Remi Montgomery?"

"She is," Merrick said. "And I'm Merrick Feingold. I work for Remi. It's like destiny, isn't it?"

"What is?" Salena asked as she waved them into the apartment. Remi noticed Salena was barefoot, so she slipped off her own shoes and set them by the door.

"I work for her. You work for Julien. It's like we belong together, right?" Merrick asked.

"Are you in love with me?" Salena asked, seemingly nonplussed by Merrick's enthusiasm.

"Not yet, but give me five or six minutes and I'll get there."

Salena nodded gracefully.

"Take your time," Salena said. She showed them to a living room. While the apartment building had appeared cramped and unremarkable on the outside, inside Remi discovered Julien's home, while not grand, was the perfect mix of classic and cozy.

"How can we help you, Miss Montgomery?"

"Please call me Remi. I'm sorry for the intrusion. I need to talk to Julien for a few minutes, and then we'll be gone."

"I'll get him for you," she said. "He's in his office."

The woman started to leave the room but paused and

turned back around. "He's mentioned you before," Salena said. "Lovely to put a face to the reputation."

"Bad reputation," Remi said, trying not to blush or wince.

"Quite the opposite," Salena said. She gave Remi a knowing smile and left the room.

"What do you think she does for Julien?" Merrick whispered after Salena had disappeared through a door.

"I don't know. She might be his assistant, so she probably does for him what you do for me."

"Annoy the piss out of you constantly and make you wish you'd never set eyes on me?" Merrick said.

"Among other useful tasks."

"She's the most beautiful woman I've ever seen in my life," Merrick said, sounding surprisingly sincere. "Can I have her?"

"She's a human being. I can't buy her for you."

"If you loved me you would help me," he said in a desperate whisper, staring at the door Salena had just passed through.

"I don't love you."

She started to pat him on the knee but paused mid-pat when Julien Brite stepped into the doorway of the living room.

"I have to say," Julien began, a crooked smile on his face, "I'm really glad my parents aren't here right now."

He looked at her, and Remi felt something catch in her chest at the sight of him leaning in his doorway, his arms crossed, and amusement glimmering in his dark eyes.

"We made sure they weren't going to be visiting you before we booked the trip," Remi said. "And hello. Nice to see you again."

"Really nice to see you again," Julien said, still smiling. He wore jeans and a plain white T-shirt, no shoes, no socks.

"How have you been, Julien?" Remi asked unable to stop staring at Julien. She hoped he didn't mind. He hadn't lost all his teenage lankiness, although his shoulders were certainly broader. His hair had darkened to a deeper shade of red and was longer now and artfully mussed. He looked older, definitely. But more than that, he looked chiseled, as if he had walked ten thousand miles across a desert and the wind and sand had worn his adolescent innocence away.

"I'm not dead," he said and laughed as if he'd made a joke. "So I'm good. You?"

"Great. Good. Also not dead."

"You're a little far from home, aren't you?" Julien asked.

"I could say the same to you," Remi said as she finally stood up and walked over to him. "Merrick said you'd moved to Paris, and I thought—"

"—Paris, Kentucky," he said. "How do you think I tricked my family into letting me move here?"

"Smart," she said.

He smiled again and held out his hand to her. Remi took it and a slight tremor passed through her body when her hand met his. The last time she'd touched him had been far more intimate than a handshake.

"I'm really sorry to show up on your doorstep," she said, Julien's hand still in hers. "I was afraid if we called first, you'd tell us to shove it."

"I am embarrassingly happy to see you again," he said, and Remi was embarrassingly relieved to hear it. "Mom said you're Arden's manager now?"

"Your mother told you about my promotion?"

"Oh yeah," Julien said, as Salena appeared in the doorway behind him. She put her hand on his hip to indicate she needed to pass by him, and he shifted the necessary six inches. The subtle gesture spoke of an intimacy between them, Salena touching his hip like that and his instant understanding that she needed him to move out of the way for her. Maybe Salena and Julien were more than mere employer and employee. "Mom keeps me up on all the Bluegrass gossip whether I want to know it or not. I know about your promotion. I know that your parents bought a satellite farm outside Versailles. I know that's your assistant Merrick Feingold sitting on my couch staring at Salena. You went to Harvard?" he asked Merrick.

"I did."

"What's a Harvard computer nerd doing working at a horse farm?" Julien asked, sounding both casual and suspicious.

"I have no people skills. It was either Wall Street or animals. And when you work for Remi Montgomery you have the sexiest boss in the world."

Merrick winked at her. It was an *I'm goading him for your sake* wink. She appreciated that.

"And how did you know I was a Harvard computer nerd?" Merrick asked. "Did my mother call you to brag?"

"Mom told me that Remi hired some Harvard computer genius who knew nothing about horses to be her assistant. And that he creeped everyone out because he wore black sunglasses all the time and was weird."

"Is 'weird' code for 'Jewish'?" Merrick asked. The sunglasses in question were currently sitting on his head.

"For my mother, yes," Julien said. "But two of my three sisters like you for some reason."

"Sisters? You have sisters? I didn't know you had sisters." Merrick whistled and looked around the apartment. "And these alleged sisters of yours must have been speaking of another Merrick Feingold. Very common name in Kentucky."

"I apologize for my assistant," Remi said to Julien. "And

me. We'll be out of your hair soon. I wanted to talk to you for about ten minutes, and then we'll leave you alone."

"You really don't have to leave me alone," Julien said. "But if you get topless again, please make sure the door's locked this time."

"Lesson learned." Remi laughed, and she knew she was blushing like a teenager in love. Luckily Julien was polite enough not to mention the blush. Unluckily Merrick wasn't.

"Stop blushing, Boss. You're the December in the May-December, remember?" Merrick said. "Wait. That rhymed."

"Merrick, you're fired," Remi said.

"Is that code for 'Merrick, please call the hotel and extend our reservations'?"

"Yes, please," Remi said.

"Thought so." Merrick pulled his phone out of his pocket. She hadn't planned on spending more than a weekend in Paris, but looking at Julien right now, it seemed the most appropriate course of action.

"Let's go to the office." Julien, slightly blushing, too, inclined his head at the door. "We can talk there. Alone." He glanced at Salena, who waved her hand to shoo him from the room.

Remi followed Julien through the doorway. Behind her she heard Merrick trying to flirt with Salena.

"You married?" Merrick asked Salena.

"My family disowned me after I refused to submit to an arranged marriage," Salena said.

"Too bad. My family disowned me, too," Merrick confessed.

"Did you also refuse a marriage?"

"No," he said. "I'm just an asshole, and no one can stand me."

"Merrick's an interesting guy," Julien said once they were out of earshot.

"He's obnoxious and bizarre. And he's flirting with your assistant."

"Salena's not my assistant."

"Girlfriend? I'll kill Merrick if you want me to. And even if you don't, I'll take any excuse at this point."

"Not my girlfriend, either. Long story." Julien pointed at an armchair. Remi glanced around. Julien had a lovely little office that was rather cramped and messy. Only two chairs and a desk graced the room, which he'd decorated with old French cinema posters. He sat on a cushioned window seat across from her; a closed curtain hung behind him. "I'm guessing you didn't hire Merrick for his knowledge of Thoroughbred racing."

"Or his charm. And not his face or body, either, despite all the rumors about us. Most days I ask myself why I hired him."

"Why did you hire him?"

"About a year ago, I started to get the feeling my parents and I were working against each other. I needed someone entirely outside the racing industry who wasn't afraid of being, you know, *sneaky* if I needed him to be. As annoying as he is, he's also brilliant and does everything I tell him to do. He helped me find you."

"Did he?"

"His brain is like a computer, and he's happy to do anything I ask him to do, especially if it's immoral or unethical—like bribing a housekeeper for your address."

"Why did you want to find me? And will I regret asking that question?" Julien grinned at her and she couldn't help but grin back. She was going to scare the boy if she didn't stop grinning.

"Probably," she admitted, forcing the smile off her face. This was business, not pleasure. "I'm here because something's rotten in the state of Kentucky. And I think our families might be involved."

CHAPTER THREE

One Kiss, Two Kiss, Red Kiss, Blue Kiss

Remi laid everything out for Julien as clearly and concisely as she could. His parents had just dropped ten million dollars on yearlings. Her parents suddenly had ten million dollars to blow on a five-hundred-acre second farm. Her father had changed the banking passwords and hadn't given her a good explanation why. If that wasn't damning enough, the private feud between the Capital Hills Brites and the Arden Farm Montgomerys had gone public this year, and it was the only story the racing press cared about. At the end of October, a Verona Downs Stakes race would take place. Six horses were entered. Shenanigans and Hijinks were the favorites. The feud and the Stakes race had even made the cover of *Sports Illustrated*. And creepy Tyson Balt had been at her parents' house and no one would talk about it.

"That doesn't sound good," Julien agreed. "I don't know much about the farm, but I do know last winter Dad said they'd budgeted for four million for yearlings."

"I triple-checked. They bought twenty-two yearlings for five million and then bought a four broodmares and four stallions—ten million total. And my parents paid cash for the farm—no mortgage. And for four years our little feud has been just between our families—and anyone who was at the Christmas party at the Rails that night. Now it's all over the news."

"Did the article mention us specifically?" Julien asked.

"No, thank God," she said. "Although it's only a matter of time before the story comes out. The article just quotes a rumor that the feud started as a lovers' quarrel."

"They can't call it a lovers' quarrel if the two lovers didn't get to be lovers."

Remi grimaced. "Better than saying the twenty-two-year-old manager of Arden Farms seduced the Brites' youngest son who was in high school."

"I have a very old soul," he said.

Remi laughed and buried her face in her hands. Between her fingers she peeked at him.

"And my very old soul had a massive erection that night."

"You're not making this any easier," she told him, lowering her hands.

"Can't help it. I'd rather talk about us than whatever our parents are into."

"Us?"

"Well…you know. What happened between us, I mean."

"Yeah, I'm sorry about that. I should have said that a long time ago."

"Don't be sorry. I'm not."

"I'm glad to hear that. I was worried you might be pissed I just showed up at your door almost four years later asking for help."

"I'll help you any way I can, Remi. It's just…it's really good to see you again."

Remi felt the heat return to her face. "You too, Julien."

They stared at each other until the silence grew heavy and awkward.

"Anyway," she said and wrenched her eyes away from him. "I am sorry to be the bearer of this shitty news."

"It's okay, I promise. I wish I could help you. I'm happy to dig around a little if I can, talk to my sisters, see if they think something weird is going on. If my parents are doing something unethical, I'd rather find out from you than from the newspapers."

"Thank you. I hate to ask you to spy on your own family."

"I haven't exactly been thrilled with my parents recently, either." Julien pulled his knee to his chest and wrapped his arm around his shin—the same arms that had once been wrapped around her.

"You moved across the ocean. That's not a great sign."

"They were asking for it," Julien said. "Two years ago when you got your promotion to farm manager, Mom said it was nepotism at its worst, that no way were you qualified to run Arden and the place would fall apart in a week. Then Arden had its best season ever. After that Mom said it was unladylike for a woman to run a horse farm. Then there were the rants about how disgusting and disgraceful it was you had an 'attractive male assistant' you were obviously sleeping with. That's when Salena and I started packing."

"You moved out just because your mom thinks Merrick and I are sleeping together?" Remi asked, astounded. "Everyone thinks Merrick and I are sleeping together except for Merrick and me."

"My issues with my parents are yet another really long story. Let's just say it was the last straw. Salena suggested we sublet a place in France for a few months. She used to live in Paris and knew I'd like it. I'm starting college again in January, so I told my parents I was getting a little place in Paris until I started school."

"Not so little," she said, glancing around what she hoped was a two-bedroom apartment. He said Salena wasn't his girlfriend, so she guessed that meant she wasn't sleeping with him. "Although I can't imagine your parents or your sisters living in a third-floor walk-up garret apartment. No offense."

"None taken," Julien said, clearly finding the idea as amusing as she did. "But, for all its downsides, this place has one very big upside."

"It is very pretty," she said.

"And it has an amazing view." Julien turned around and opened the curtain behind him that had shielded the window.

"Holy…" Remi rose out of her seat and walked to the window. Julien moved to the side and Remi sat next to him on the bench.

Through a gap in the buildings she could see the top of the Eiffel Tower in all its illuminated nighttime glory. She stared at it in silence and sensed Julien's eyes on her, not the tower in the distance. Four years evaporated in an instant. Four years ago they were talking by the fireplace and now a window overlooking Paris. Four years come and gone in an instant.

"I used to dream about living in Paris," she said after a long pause. She couldn't quite believe that she was here in Paris with Julien Brite gazing at the Eiffel Tower. It was perfect—the autumn air of the city pressing against the window, the lights dancing on the tower, Julien at her side looking at her and nothing else. Not just perfect but a perfect moment—why did she keep having these with him? "When I was a little girl. Too many Madeline books, I guess."

"Who?"

"It's a girl thing." Remi gazed at the top of the tower,

wondering what the city looked like from the top. Maybe she would see it before they left. Maybe Julien could take her there tomorrow.

"What did you dream about?" Julien asked. He kept his voice low, as if the entire city were trying to listen in but he wanted to keep their conversation between only them.

"Oh, the usual kid dreams. Living in Paris, speaking French, eating croissants all the time."

"They are pretty amazing here," Julien agreed.

"Then I got older, and I still dreamed of Paris. When I was a teenager it seemed like the most romantic place in the world. I wanted to get my first kiss in Paris. Which, sadly, did not happen."

"Where did you get your first kiss?"

"In the Kentucky Theater in Lexington. Not nearly as romantic as Paris. You?"

"Um…the Capitol building, actually. School field trip. Some girl in my class thought it would be rebellious to make out in the Capitol Rotunda. The statue of Abraham Lincoln was watching us. Not romantic. A first kiss in Paris with the Eiffel Tower watching us would have been much better."

"Definitely," she said, smiling. When she turned her eyes back to Julien, she found him still looking at her. He wasn't smiling, but the look on his face was better than a smile.

"Can I tell you something crazy?" she asked.

"Please. The crazier the better."

"I look for you at every race," she confessed. "Kentucky. California. New York. Florida. Doesn't matter what the race is, what track we're at, I always look for your face in the crowd, in the clubhouse, in the stands. You'd think after all this time I would quit looking for you. Is that crazy?"

He shook his head. "Not as crazy as me writing you letters that I've never worked up the courage to send."

"Letters?"

"Real ones. Ink on paper."

"Why did you never send them?" she asked, hoping he still had the letters. "I wanted to write you, too, or call you, or anything. But I was the older one and my parents forbade me from contacting you at all in case your parents got cops and lawyers involved."

"I didn't send them because I didn't think you'd want to read them." Julien took a heavy breath. "I convinced myself I was just a stupid love-struck kid and no way would this beautiful older woman want to hear from me. Especially with everything that had happened."

"I would have loved to have heard from you, I promise. Even if it was just to tell me you were okay. I worried about you after that night."

"You did? How come?"

"I don't know. Just a feeling I had. I couldn't shake it. I saw your sisters at the races but never you. It was like you disappeared after Christmas. Maybe that's why I kept looking for you at every race I went to. Or maybe I just really like your face."

She raised her hand and stroked his cheek. His skin felt warm—not feverish, simply heated. If he touched her face right now he, too, would feel her raised temperature just from the proximity of their bodies. She lowered her hand, afraid to touch him any further.

"That night at the party," Julien said, "I thought you were the most beautiful woman I'd ever seen in my life. How is it possible you're even more beautiful now?"

She knew she should say something, anything to dispel the anticipation, the tension that buzzed in the air between them. Their families were in a very public feud. Their families weren't just families but businesses. Getting involved with Julien could lead to accusations of collusion. Real ugly consequences. She needed to take a step back from Julien. Maybe two. Three would be best. Actually she should get on a plane and head straight for Kentucky.

Right now.

She kissed him.

Julien didn't seem the least surprised she kissed him. When their lips met he opened his mouth and let his tongue graze her tongue. She felt the kiss all the way from her lips to her toes and back up again.

Remi pulled back before the kiss turned into more than a kiss. She'd been down that dangerous road before.

"I didn't mean to do that," Remi said.

"You didn't?" Julien asked, looking flushed and bright-eyed.

"No. Really. I was thinking in my head all the reasons I shouldn't kiss you and then…"

"I was thinking the same thing," he said. "Thinking that our parents' worst nightmare would be you and I getting involved and so we should absolutely not get involved."

"You're right. You're completely right."

"But I'm going to kiss you anyway," Julien said.

"Thank God."

He cupped the back of her neck and brought his mouth to hers. The second kiss was even more passionate than the first.

Julien kissed her like he'd die if he didn't, like he hadn't been kissed in a decade, like he had a gun to the back of his head and had been ordered to kiss her as if his life depended on it.

She wrapped her arms around his shoulders and pushed her breasts against his chest. She dug her hand into the back of his hair and found it silky and soft. Julien's hand was on her thigh over her skirt, creating a thousand wicked images in her head. He could lift her skirt, pull off her panties, and bury himself inside her right now. And they could do it and she wouldn't feel at all guilty about it, because he wasn't in high school anymore and his parents were across an ocean.

They paused long enough to look at each other for confirmation that they could and would continue. In the distance, the lights on the Eiffel Tower turned to blue. And in the haze of blue light their lips met again.

Julien ran his hand down the center of her back. Remi held him even closer, tighter to her body.

This is crazy. This is wrong.

Those words bounced about her brain as they kissed, but they touched neither her body nor her heart. Yes, it was crazy. Yes, it was wrong. And no, that wasn't about to stop her.

She stopped only long enough to take a breath.

The Eiffel Tower turned red.

"What on earth?"

"Light show," Julien said. "They do it every night. But we can pretend it's just for us if you want."

"I want. God, I want."

She wanted to kiss him again and so she did. Or perhaps he kissed her this time. What did it matter who kissed whom as long as the kiss never ended? For four years they'd had this unfinished business hanging between them. Maybe they should finish it.

"I missed you," Julien said against her lips. "I kept trying to forget you, and I couldn't."

"I think of you every Christmas," she whispered back. "Christmas hasn't been the same since that night. No matter what I get, it's never what I want."

"What do you want?" Julien asked, and she knew he wasn't asking about Christmas gifts.

"Another shot at Christmas with you," she whispered.

She rested her forehead against his. One minute. All she needed was one minute of not kissing to clear her head so she could think straight.

"Julien, if we get involved, our parents are going to kill us," she said. "I'm not saying we shouldn't get involved. I'm just saying there will be consequences."

"My mother thinks it's shameful Arden Farms has a female manager. My father routinely calls you a slut. And your family and my family are somehow making millions of dollars off a staged horse rivalry. You think I care what they think?"

"Yes," she said. "Same way I care about what my parents think, because they love me and I love them even if they are pissing me the hell off right now."

"I care too," he admitted. "But not enough to stop kissing you."

"No more kissing until we get to your bedroom. You kiss me again like that, and we'll never make it."

"Kiss you like what?" he asked as he half-dragged her from the bench.

"Kiss me like you haven't kissed anybody in a really long time and you need to make up for lost time."

"Would it completely freak you out if I told you that was true?"

"No, of course not. We all have dry spells."

"This is a little more than a dry spell," Julien said, looking sheepish. She knew that look. Julien had worn that same expression right before confessing he was only seventeen.

"What is it, Julien? You can tell me."

"That's kind of a long story."

"You have a lot of long stories. You ran away from Kentucky and moved to Paris to get away from your parents. You have an assistant who isn't your assistant but who lives with you. And you've had more than a dry spell? What's going on? Tell me."

"'Dry spell' is an understatement," he said.

"Oh shit." Remi covered her mouth with her hand.

"Don't ask," he said, a look of quiet desperation in his eyes. "Please."

"Oh my God."

"I have a good excuse, I swear."

"You're a virgin?" she asked, utterly astounded.

"I asked you not to ask." Julien crossed his arms over his chest and laughed nervously.

"I'm sorry."

"Does it really bother you?"

"I'm just shocked," Remi said, looking at Julien in a new light.

"Shocked?"

"You're beautiful, Julien. I thought that the second I saw you four years ago. I thought that the second I saw you again tonight. And now you're blushing and you're even sexier than you were four seconds ago."

"Let's go talk in my room. There's something I need to tell you. And show you."

"Your naked body?"

"If you still want to see it after I tell you everything, then you can see it."

"The 'if' was not necessary, I promise," she said.

Julien took her hand and led her through the now empty living room.

"Wonder where Merrick and Salena went?" Julien whispered.

"It's Merrick. Five bucks says they're in her bedroom."

"Salena's really picky about the guys she dates."

"It's Merrick. Trust me, this isn't about dating."

Julien took her hand and they crept past a closed door. They heard a voice from within.

"So how old are you?" they heard Merrick asking Salena.

"Thirty-three. You?" Salena asked.

"Thirty-six. You put us together and you get sixty-nine."

"You're very good at math."

"Who was doing math?" Merrick asked.

"Mystery solved," Julien whispered and rolled his eyes. He looked so cute with his amused disgust that Remi had to stop herself from grabbing his face and kissing him again. "Let's go."

They quickly reached his room at the end of the hall. He pushed the door open and ripped a small folded piece of paper off the door. He glanced at the note, smiled and shoved it into his pocket. As soon as they were in the room with the door locked behind them, Julien pulled her to him. Remi raised her hand and covered his mouth.

"No kissing. You talk to me first," she said.

"My man't malk wiff your mand on my mouff."

"What?" she asked, pulling her hand back.

"I can't talk with your hand on my mouth," Julien said.

"Okay, you talk. I'll be sitting at a safe distance and listening." Remi picked up a chair and set it five feet from the bed, where Julien now sat. She was impressed by his bedroom. The walls were an elegant jade green and the bed frame an antique brass. The walls were lined with beautiful if bizarre art, and every surface was spotless.

"Your room is really clean," she said. "That's not natural."

"Salena hired a housekeeper. Was not my idea. I'm not that spoiled."

"I want to know about Salena. She's way too beautiful, she lives with you, but she's not your assistant and yet she hired a housekeeper."

"And she's seen me naked. A lot. Just making sure you know everything."

"I hope there's a good explanation for that." Remi wasn't the jealous type, but she was quickly getting used to the idea of being the only woman who got to see Julien naked.

"There is. And it has everything to do with why, I'm, you know…"

"Undefiled?"

"That's a diplomatic word for a guy who's never gotten laid."

"I'm trying to be diplomatic. It's better than ripping your clothes off," Remi said, and sat on her hands to remind herself to let him talk before the clothes-ripping began.

"I'd rather you just rip my clothes off."

"Talk," she ordered.

"Okay, I'm talking. It's just… It sort of changes everything when I bring it up."

"Bring what up? What is it?"

"The reason I'm a virgin and the reason Salena lives with me and the reason I have a housekeeper who keeps everything spotless and disinfected and the reason I lived with my parents until last year when I finally couldn't stand it anymore and the reason I didn't send you all the letters I wrote you…"

"What's the reason?"

Julien took a deep breath. He seemed to be steeling himself. "Salena's not my assistant, but she does work for us."

"What does she do?"

"She's my doctor. Dr. Salena Kar—oncologist."

Remi's mouth fell open. She quickly closed it. Her desire for Julien turned instantly to pity, compassion and fear.

"You have a live-in oncologist?" she whispered.

"I do."

"What do you have?"

Julien sighed again. "It's not what I have. It's what I had."

"Which was?"

"Leukemia, Remi. Two weeks after you and I almost had sex, I was diagnosed with leukemia."

CHAPTER FOUR

No Last Names

"Leukemia," Remi repeated. Her mouth formed the word but her tongue wanted to spit it back out, reject the word, the truth, the suffering, Julien had experienced.

"Acute myeloid leukemia, if you want to be specific."

"That sounds…bad."

Julien laughed a little. "There's no good leukemia."

"No," Remi breathed, her hands shaking from shock. "I wouldn't think so. What happened?"

Julien shrugged and sighed. She knew he didn't want to tell the story but she had to hear it. Every word.

"The night of the Christmas party, you thought I was older than I was. Why?"

"I don't know," she said. "You were almost six feet tall and had a glass of wine in your hand."

"I thought it was probably the wine that made you think I was older."

"That and how intelligent and funny you were. I'm surprised your parents let you drink wine."

"They usually didn't. But I had a headache that day. It got

worse at the party. Dad said I could have one glass of wine and if that didn't help I should just go lie down in one of the guest bedrooms. They'd find me when it was time to go. That's why Mom was looking for me."

"You didn't tell me you had a headache that night."

"I'd had a headache off and on for a week. When I saw you and we started talking, it disappeared. But it came back the next day. A week after Christmas, I started getting bruises that wouldn't heal. I finally told Mom I thought something was wrong with me, and I showed her the bruises on my stomach. Next day I'm in the doctor's office getting blood drawn and my mom's crying and the doctor's looking at my blood in the tube and scowling."

"Scowling is not good," Remi said, her hands shaking as if it had been her in that room next to Julien watching a doctor stick a needle in his arm.

"The doctor said he was going to run some tests, and I should pray I got an A on the tests."

"An A?"

"A for is for Anemia, which is easy to treat and would have explained the bruises and the headaches. I got a C on my test instead. Cancer. They admitted me into the hospital immediately. Then home for a few days. Then I was back in the hospital again. After the bone marrow transplant, I pretty much lived in the hospital."

"How bad was it?"

"Bad," he said simply. "But it's always bad. With cancer it's either bad or worse. Mine was bad, so it could have been worse. That's what you tell yourself to make it through the night. Mine was treatable, even curable. Not all of the big Cs are."

Her heart ground against the gears of her chest. Julien spoke of his years at death's doorway so casually, too casually.

"So you're better? Completely?"

"See that?" Julien pointed to a chart on the wall. "That's a five-year calendar. Declared in total remission one year and eleven months ago. That's when the countdown starts. At five years if I'm still clear, then I'm cured. But the likelihood of relapse is extremely low at this point."

"Good," she said and exhaled a breath she hadn't known she'd been holding.

"But you should know, there are some lingering issues. I'd get Salena in here to tell you all the dirty details, but I think she's a little busy right now."

Remi stood up and walked over to his bed. She touched the side of his face. "I want *you* to tell me, no one else."

He shrugged and rolled onto his back. Not able to stay away from him any longer, she stretched out on her side next to him. Julien stared up at the ceiling. She stared at Julien.

"Okay, dirty details. Leukemia sucks. I lived in the hospital for months at a time. Radiation makes you skeletal. No teenage guy wants to weigh ninety pounds. Then you get chemo and steroids and you blow up like a balloon. Skeletal. Fat. Skeletal. Fat. I banned cameras. There are literally zero pictures of me from age seventeen to nineteen in existence."

"I was wondering why I never found any pictures of you. Your family's in the news all the time."

"Even when I was having good days, feeling okay, Mom wouldn't let me out of the house. All the treatments kill the immune system."

"House arrest?"

"Basically," Julien said. "Not her fault. Mom and Dad never talked about me being sick to anyone because I asked them not to, and they respected that."

"You were sick. That's nothing to be embarrassed about."

"I know that now. Harder to accept when you're seventeen and bald and there are days you can't even go to the bathroom without help. I didn't want visitors. I didn't want people all over me. I just wanted to get through it and get on with my life."

"I can see that, but still…God, if I'd known you were sick, I would never have let my family say a word about your family even around our kitchen table. This stupid feud would have been over even if I had to tie up, gag and chain every last relative and throw them in the basement."

"Kinky," Julien said. Remi flicked him in the arm. "Sorry."

"Don't be," Remi said. "Just keep talking. I want to know everything."

"This next part is embarrassing."

"Tell me, Julien. Please tell me everything."

"I'm sterile," Julien said. He glanced her way before staring assiduously at the ceiling again.

"You mean, *sterile* sterile? Permanently?"

"Chemotherapy plus bone marrow transplant means goodbye to your fertility forever. It's possible I could have kids someday. They froze some of my sperm."

"That was smart." She was saying things she knew she should say, keeping calm, being rational even as her stomach roiled with unspoken emotion—grief, sadness, relief… so much relief that he had lived to tell his tale.

"Smart and horrible. Talk about humiliating, sitting in front of your doctor with your mom next to you and discussing your sperm."

"Oh God, you poor thing." Remi could have cried at the thought of what Julien had endured. She felt an ache, almost physical, to go back in time and somehow be there for him and with him while he'd gone through it all.

"Yeah, that was a bad day." He laughed softly and rubbed

his forehead. "I don't think Mom's ever recovered from the 'Save Julien's sperm' conversation, either. Anyway, thought you should know that part up front."

"My horses are my babies. I don't need much else," she said before realizing they were already talking about the future. Where had this come from? She didn't know. Right now she didn't care. "That doesn't bother me."

"Seriously?"

"Seriously. Anything else I need to know?" she asked.

"Nothing much more to tell. Oh, except this. Two years after diagnosis I'm finally in remission. After about six months after that I started to feel pretty normal. I looked normal, too. My hair was back. It was short but at least I had some. I couldn't wait to get out of the house. I was starting college and was so ready to have a girlfriend."

"And have sex?" she teased.

"All the sex," he said.

"So what happened?"

"My immune system still wasn't one hundred percent. I caught a cold. The cold turned into pneumonia. I had to take a medical leave from school two months in. I've never been back to school. College dropout. Thank God for trust funds, right?"

"Why didn't you go back to school when you were better?"

"Mom took the pneumonia as a sign I should be in lockdown. Do you know how hard it is to meet women when your mother won't let you out of your own house? And it's really hard to kiss someone when you're under orders to wear a surgical mask."

"You had to wear surgical masks?"

"Everyone in the house wore them around me," Julien said. "And that's where Salena comes in. My parents hired

Salena to be my live-in doctor. Salena had burnout and student loans from med school. My parents paid off her loans,
and now she has only the one patient. Well, two patients
counting Mom. First thing Salena did was diagnose my
mother with 'vulnerable child syndrome.' Real syndrome. It's
basically pathological overprotectiveness. And then she wrote
Mom a prescription. Four words—'Let Julien move out.'"

Remi would have applauded if her hand had been free.

"Thank God for Salena. That's really smart, writing it on
a prescription pad."

"Doctor's orders," Julien said. "Salena writes me prescriptions all the time. 'Go running' or 'Go hiking' or 'Ask her
out on a date.'"

"She writes you prescriptions for dates?"

"She's awesome, right? I had to have a ton of tests and stuff
to get cleared to have sex. You know, they had to make sure
my immune system could take it. Salena did all the tests and
then after I got cleared, she sat me in her office and gave me
a three-hour lecture on sex, women and the female anatomy. She had charts and diagrams. The films were my favorite part. It was amazing. I've never had sex, but I know
where the clitoris and the G-spot are, and I know what to
do when I find them."

"Can I go kiss Salena now? On the mouth?"

"Can I watch?" Julien asked.

"Of course."

"I love Salena," Julien said with a wide-eyed exhalation.
"She's my hero and my best friend. She rescued me from my
own house, makes me go out, have a life, try new things."

"Like moving to Paris?"

"Once I was cleared for 'adult activities,' as Salena calls
them, she staged an intervention with my parents and told
them they were making things worse by keeping me cooped

up and treating me like I was on death's doorstep. My parents worship doctors, so they took her seriously and let me go. I just had to take Salena with me so she could monitor my medical condition."

"So you ran off to Paris?"

"I said Paris. They assumed Paris, Kentucky. I didn't exactly correct them."

"Did they freak out?" Remi asked.

"They did at first. But Salena talked sense into them. France has the best health-care system in the world. Much better than the U.S. And I'm healthy as a horse now. Salena makes sure of that."

"I'm happy to hear that." Remi realized she might have made the understatement of the century. "Ecstatic" would have been more accurate.

"My parents are calmer now about the Paris thing. Salena loves it here. I love it here. Been learning the language, trying to meet people."

"Meet women?"

Julien shrugged. "Been on a few dates."

"Only a few?"

Julien gave her a crooked smile and a halfhearted chuckle. "Did you know *cancer* is the same word in English and in French? No matter what language, the word sends girls running. It's not that it's in the past. That's not what scares people. It's that it can come back. It might come back. Anytime I get a headache, a cold, anything, my family freaks out. Anybody who is in my life will share in that fear. Hard to ask that much courage from someone you just met, right? No wonder the girls go running when I tell them the truth."

Remi rose up and looked down at Julien, still lying on his back on the bed.

"I'm not running," she said.

"Why not?" Julien asked.

"I am the least romantic person I've ever known," she confessed. "But for some reason…"

She said no more because she knew she didn't have to.

"I know," Julien said in a low voice, almost scared.

"I've never forgotten you. I should have. You were seventeen. I'd just graduated college that December. I should have gotten over you a long time ago. I never did. And now that I'm here with you, I feel like this is exactly where I'm supposed to be."

"Although it ended badly, I was so grateful we had that moment at the Christmas party. Those nights I was alone in the hospital with nothing but my fears and my exhaustion, and I thought maybe I would just stop fighting, go to sleep and never wake up again, I would remember that night with you. I remembered kissing you, touching you, being touched by you…and it helped me keep my eyes on the future. A future where I was healthy again and wasn't alone. You were with me the whole time, Remi."

Remi blinked back tears. Neither of them spoke. A heavy, meaningful silence descended. She didn't want to rush things, didn't want to push him. But for all her noble intentions, she also wanted to kiss him again, touch every inch of him, and spend all night with him in this bed helping him make up for lost time and show him exactly what he'd been fighting for.

"This is going to sound like a line," Julien finally said, "but I swear it isn't. The thing is…when you spend age seventeen to nineteen thinking you might die, it changes the way you look at your life. I decided I wanted to move to Paris on a Thursday. Salena and I were on a plane Monday. When you want to do something, you do it. You don't wait a week, a year. Because you know you might not be around next year, next week."

"Carpe diem?" Remi asked.

"That means 'seize the day,'" Julien said. "It's night."

"Carpe... Hold on a second. Merrick?" she called out loudly, loud enough she knew her voice carried throughout the entire apartment.

"Little busy, Boss!" he yelled back, his voice easily penetrating the wall of Julien's bedroom.

"What's Latin for 'night'?"

"Depends on the part of speech!"

"Direct object!"

"Noctem!" he yelled.

"Thank you!" Remi shouted. Then she turned to Julien and whispered, *"Carpe noctem.* 'Seize the night.'"

"We could have just looked that up online," Julien said.

"I know. But I wanted a little payback for all the times Merrick starts conversations with me when I'm in the bathroom. Plus, what's the point in having a genius assistant who knows Latin without asking him to help you with it?"

"Good point."

"So..." Remi said as that tense, taut silence descended on the room again. She slid her hand up and down the center of Julien's chest. With each pass down his stomach she moved lower. Under her hand she felt his stomach fluttering. Julien was nervous. She liked that.

"So..." Julien said. "What do you want to do?"

"It's your decision," she said. "You have more to lose than I do."

"Literally," he said.

"How about this? How about I kiss you right now and you kiss me back and we'll keep kissing until something more happens or we fall asleep?"

"I like that idea. And, you know, *carpe noctem.*"

She nodded and whispered, "Seize the night."

Remi leaned over Julien and brought her lips to his.

Julien slid his fingers through her hair and pulled her even closer as the kiss deepened. The position was uncomfortable enough that Remi felt entirely justified in yanking her skirt to her knees and straddling Julien's thighs. Julien inhaled sharply.

"I don't weigh too much, do I?" Remi asked, freezing. She was no waif by any stretch of the imagination. At five-nine with muscles and curves, she might have weighed more than Julien.

"You weigh the perfect amount and the perfect amount of you came in contact with a certain part of me. Please do it again."

Remi laughed and settled in on top of him. The kissing, at first tentative, quickly turned torrid. Julien might not have done much kissing in his life, but Remi had no complaints about his technique. She couldn't get enough of his mouth, nor he hers. Julien rolled them onto their sides without breaking the kiss. He slipped his hand under her shirt and caressed her back. She wanted to feel his skin too, as much of it as she could. She slid her hand under his T-shirt and rubbed his side. He was so warm and young and eager. If he wanted, kissing would only be the beginning of their night together.

"You smell like roses," Julien whispered into her neck as he nibbled under her ear.

"It's my soap."

"It's not your soap, it's your skin. It's all of you," he said, his hand now at the center of her back, teasing the expanse between her shoulder blades.

"If you're trying to seduce me, it's working." Remi pushed her hips into his. Pressure had already started to build inside her.

"I thought you were trying to seduce me," Julien teased.

"I can if you want me to."

"I'd love to see what you try," he said, a wicked grin on his face. She adored that face, adored those eyes that shone so bright with desire.

"Let's see, when we were last alone together in a bedroom, I believe I was…"

She came up on her knees and unbuttoned her blouse. Julien reached out and helped pull her shirt down her arms. She threw it onto the floor with a flourish. Julien knelt in front of her and kissed the tops of her breasts. She forced herself to do nothing as he kissed her neck and chest. They shouldn't rush things. This night could be Julien's first time. He'd spent his teen years fighting for his life. Why not show him exactly how much light had been waiting for him at the end of that tunnel?

"You're really okay, now?" Remi asked, as Julien wrapped his arms around her back and pulled her even closer. They faced each other on their knees, her breasts pressing against his chest. She could feel his heart pounding.

"I'm fine. You're not going to hurt me, I promise."

"Good," she said and pushed him down onto his back. He laughed as she straddled him again. But the laughter stopped the moment she unhooked her bra and took it off. She took him by his wrists and brought his hands to her breasts.

"Oh my God," he said, holding her breasts, squeezing and cupping them. "I've missed them so much."

Remi laughed but the laugh abruptly turned to a gasp when Julien pinched her nipples. A shock of pleasure bolted through her from her breasts to her back and all the way down her spine. Her nipples hardened as Julien teased them and gently tugged them. She closed her eyes and did nothing but let Julien touch her. She felt his erection pressing against her, even through his jeans.

"Your turn," she said breathlessly. "I don't want to be the only shirtless person in the room."

"Okay, but…"

She shook her head. "No butts yet. Just your shirt."

Remi sat back so Julien could roll up. He sighed heavily before pulling his shirt off over his head.

"It's not as bad as it looks," he said, lying on his back again.

Remi gazed down at his chest. He was thin, yes. Thin but muscular. He'd clearly taken getting into shape very seriously after his recovery. He had a taut stomach, sinewy biceps, a broad chest, and…

"No," she said. "It's not bad at all."

She reached out and touched the raised four-inch scar on the right-hand side of his upper chest. It was smooth and bright pink, much like Julien's face at the moment.

"They put this thing in your chest—a MediPort," he explained. "It's how the drugs are delivered."

"Then I'm glad you have the scar. It saved your life."

"The day they took it out was the best day of my life. Until today."

Remi's fingers fluttered. When had she ever desired someone this much?

"It's hideous I know," Julien said, wincing slightly.

"It's not bad at all."

"Good. You can keep staring at it. It'll give me an excuse to stare at you."

Remi put her hands on either side of his shoulders and lay on top of him. When her bare breasts touched his naked chest, he inhaled sharply.

"You okay?" she asked.

"I'm so happy I'm not dead right now, I could cry," he said. "Am I dead? Is this heaven? Can you get erections in heaven?"

"Wouldn't be heaven otherwise." Remi stretched out on

her back so Julien could have total access to her chest. They kissed again as he ran his hand over both her breasts, gently touching, squeezing, holding, caressing. He lightly pinched her nipples between his thumb and forefinger. His touch gave her breathtaking amounts of pleasure. As he touched her, she slid her hand up and down his arm, relishing the ridges of muscle he'd worked so hard for after recovering.

Remi threw her leg over Julien's hip to bring his body even closer to hers.

He closed his eyes tight as if he were in pain.

"I am seriously turned on right now," he said. "Sorry."

"Don't say you're sorry. Do you want to stop or keep going?"

"Keep going. Definitely."

"Are you saying that because you mean it or because you're turned on?"

"*Both* is my answer," he said. "If that's the right answer."

"There is no right or wrong answer. It's whatever you want," she said, running her hand through his hair again and stroking the side of his face.

"I want you." Julien took her chin in his hand and caressed her bottom lip with his thumb. "I want you so much it hurts. But..."

"I know," she said. "If our families find out about this, we're dead."

"Very dead. And me and death were on speaking terms not that long ago. I know death. They'll kill us."

"Whatever our parents are up to, they need the press to think both families hate each other." Remi knew this public rivalry was making them all a fortune.

"And they do hate each other," Julien said. "They just love money more."

"So what do we do?" Remi asked, aching at the thought

of walking away from Julien so soon after finding him. "We can't just pretend I'm not a Montgomery and you're not a Brite."

"Maybe we can for one night," he said. "You're just Remi. I'm just Julien. No last names."

Remi grinned at him. Not a bad idea. Whatever they did tonight was no one's business but theirs. Why should it matter what their last names were? She had only one more question.

"Okay, Just-Julien, now what do you want to do?"

CHAPTER FIVE

Carpe Noctem

"Maybe we should follow the doctor's orders," Julien said with a sly smile.

"Doctor's orders?" Remi asked.

Julien pulled the paper out of his pocket that had been taped to the door. He unfolded it and showed it to her. It was a prescription pad for Dr. Salena Kar—Oncologist. And the good Dr. Kar had prescribed a very special medicine for Julien.

"SEX," it read in all caps. The one and only word on it.

"Well, she *is* the doctor," Remi said.

Julien threw the note in the air and wrapped both arms around Remi. He pressed Remi onto the bed, and lightly gripped her wrists. He kissed her from her neck to her breasts and drew a nipple into his mouth and sucked it gently.

"That is such a good idea, Just-Julien," she sighed with relief, his choice made. He wanted her as much as she wanted him. "Whoever you are."

"I'm nobody," he whispered against her skin. "I'm just a random guy you met in Paris."

"I was here for a vacation," she said as he kissed his way across her chest to her other nipple. "I work my ass off."

"You needed a vacation," Julien said. "And I need your ass." He playfully cupped her bottom and squeezed.

"I did. And while on vacation I saw a gorgeous younger man walking down the street."

"How gorgeous?"

"Beyond gorgeous. Striking. Not normal gorgeous. Different."

"Different? Are you talking about me or Merrick?"

"In this fantasy I've never met Merrick, which is why it's the best fantasy I've ever had."

Julien laughed before taking her nipple into his mouth again. She moaned as the heat seeped into her skin and sent delicious shivers all the way to the pit of her stomach. Her clitoris was swelling. She couldn't stop her hips from moving against Julien.

"So what else about this guy?" Julien asked as he palmed her breast.

"I'm not sure. I feel like I've known him all my life. Usually I don't jump into bed this fast with a guy, but he seems special. And not just because of the aforementioned striking-ness."

"Is that a word?"

"It is now. But I think maybe this is something...I don't know."

"I know," Julien said, looking up at her. "I feel it, too. Like this was meant to happen, and we have to let it happen."

"Do you want it to happen?" she asked.

Julien nodded.

"Then we'll let it happen," she said, her voice as soft and tender as the look on Julien's face. And she knew they weren't talking about sex anymore. Not only sex, anyway. But them.

The future. Whatever it meant. They would let it happen. Their hearts left them no other choice.

No more words were exchanged. No more words were needed. Julien stood up and Remi pulled the covers back on the bed. She rested on her back, propped on her elbows, and watched Julien undress. He didn't hesitate, not even when the moment came to take his boxer briefs off.

He had a beautiful young body and she devoured the sight of it. Once Julien was naked, she unzipped her skirt in the back. Julien pulled her skirt down her legs and tossed it to the floor. She had on nothing but her panties now. Julien crawled onto the bed and stretched out on top of her.

Remi reached between their bodies and wrapped her hand around his erection. She stroked upward as Julien closed his eyes.

"I remember that," he said, as she ran her fingers from the wet tip to the base and back up again. She touched him lightly at first and then gripped him firmly with her entire hand.

"You remember me touching you like this?"

"It's better than I remembered, Remi. It's better than I dreamed. And I dreamed this moment so many times."

His eyes were closed and soft breaths escaped his slightly parted lips. She dipped her head and took him in her mouth.

"And I remember that too," he said, panting between breaths.

"Tell me what you dreamed," she said before taking him in her mouth again. She was gentle, slow. She wanted to keep him hard but not make him come yet.

"What I dreamed?" He sounded dazed and breathless. Remi flicked her tongue over the tip and he flinched. One way to get his attention. She sat back up again and rubbed him with her hand.

"When I was a teenager," she said, "I used to dream about what my first time would be like. And then it happened and it wasn't a dream come true. Tell me what you want, and maybe we can make your dream come true."

"Remi…"

"Tell me, please," she said. "Let me do this for you."

Julien exhaled and opened his eyes.

"I had a ton of fantasies. They were great distractions from real life. Real life sucked for a long time."

"How did you want it to happen?"

"In my bed," he said. "No fancy hotels, no castles or anything. When you're in the hospital, your own bed becomes this symbol—home. Not just home but home free. When they let you go home for good, it's because you're better. So being in my own bed at home would mean I was good, out of the woods. And that was a very sexy thought."

"Here we are, in your own bed. Anything else?" she asked as she kissed his neck.

"I liked the thought of being on my back for the first time. But when you're seventeen all you want to do is see breasts. Everywhere. All the time."

"That can be arranged," she murmured against his skin. "What else?"

"I dreamed…" he said and paused. "This is stupid."

"Tell me anyway."

"I dreamed that my first time would be with someone who was really happy to be my first time. And second. And third."

"It's a good dream," she said, running a hand down the center of his back. "I'm thrilled to be your first time and can't wait for the second and third. So let's make your dream come true."

Remi held her breath as Julien eased her panties down her legs. She was nervous, which made no sense. He was the virgin, not her. But that was the reason, the one remaining rational part of her brain told her. She was nervous for Julien. She wanted him to enjoy every second of his first time. After all he'd been through, after what he'd survived, she wanted his first time to be perfect.

She kicked her underwear off her ankle and opened her legs for him. He slid his hand up her thigh as he looked at her. The only light in the room came from the bedside lamp and the streetlights streaming in through the window. But it was light enough for him to see every part of her.

"Good? Bad? Weird?" she asked, as he traced the seam of her labia with his fingertip.

"Amazing," he breathed. Remi smiled and settled deep into his bed and let him touch her. First he caressed her outer lips with his fingertips. When she whispered a desperate "Please, Julien," he pushed one finger inside her. He closed his eyes as if wanting to focus solely on his sense of touch. "You're so wet inside. And warm."

"I'm turned on. That's what happens to women when we get turned on."

"I know. Dr. Salena gave me the lowdown on your down-lows," he said.

"My down-lows are grateful to the good doctor."

"God, you feel so good. I want you turned on like this all the time forever and ever," he said, opening his eyes again.

"Amen," Remi said. "I don't know if that was a prayer or not, but I'm amen-ing anyway."

He pushed in a second finger, and she sighed with pleasure and need. He went in deep and pulled out again, in and out, as she grew even wetter and hotter on the inside.

She opened her legs even wider, and Julien pushed in a third finger. Remi gasped with pleasure, and Julien froze.

"Don't stop," she said. "That sound I made is the opposite of me telling you to stop. Memorize it."

He nodded and pushed his three fingers into her again, in deep. She felt full and open, but not uncomfortably so. She wanted him to experience all of her, inside and out. He explored her with his fingertips, running them up and down the front wall. He hit a spot inside her, and Remi gasped loudly.

"Good?" he asked.

"Do it again," she begged.

"Yes, ma'am," he said, laughing.

He massaged her G-spot, pressing into it with gentle spirals that sent Remi's hips rising off the bed. She grabbed the brass bar of the headboard behind her. So much tension built in Remi that she had to breathe deeply and slowly to keep from coming right then and there on Julien's hand. It felt so good, she wasn't ready for it to end yet. She'd had good sex before. Even great sex. But she'd never felt this open before, never been this wet and this aroused, and never wanted someone inside her so much in her life.

"What do you want me to do?" Julien asked, his voice as breathless as hers. "I want you to come."

"I'm really close," she panted.

"Tell me what you like," he said. He looked down at her with his dark eyes shining, his skin flushed, his lips wet and parted. She rose up and kissed him, needing to taste his mouth again.

She reached between her legs and pulled his hand out of her. With her hand over his hand she guided him to her clitoris.

"There," she said. "Kissing here or touching here is how the magic happens."

"I want to make the magic happen," he said, lightly

gripping her clitoris between his thumb and forefinger to knead it.

"That"—Remi collapsed onto her back again—"is magical."

She could feel her clitoris swelling even more under his touch. Lost as she was in the ecstasy, she barely noticed him sliding down the bed until she felt his tongue on her. He pushed three fingers back into her as he sucked on the tight knot. Remi twined her fingers through his soft hair and held his neck gently as he pumped his fingers into her and licked her simultaneously. No amount of deep breathing could stop her from coming now. Her entire body went stiff and still for what felt like an eternity as Julien lapped at her with the hunger of a starving man.

With one hoarse cry, Remi came, her inner muscles fluttering hard and deep inside her, the muscles twitching around Julien's fingers, her clitoris throbbing against his tongue.

"Stop," she said, and Julien immediately pulled his fingers from her and sat up.

"You okay?" He sounded almost scared.

"I am not okay. I am amazing." She slowly opened her eyes. "Except I'm sure that orgasm was loud enough Merrick heard it. Work is going to be awkward from now on."

Julien laughed. "I think he's distracted." He tilted his head and Remi heard the unmistakable sound of a headboard rhythmically hitting a wall. "There is a lot of sex happening in this apartment tonight."

"Ah, Paris," Remi said, smiling like the world's happiest drunk. "Either Paris makes people have better orgasms or Dr. Salena taught you well."

"That was the sexiest thing ever," Julien said, cupping her breast with his wet fingers. Her nipples had grown more sensitive with arousal. The heat from his hand seeped deep into her skin. She never wanted him to stop touching her.

"It's not always easy to make a woman orgasm. You should be proud of yourself."

"I plan on doing it again as soon as you let me." Julien pinched her nipple and rolled it between his fingers.

"Now it's your turn," she said, laying a hand on the side of his face. "Ready?"

Julien heaved a breath and nodded. A slight tremor passed through his body. Her heart galloped inside her chest at the look of trust and need on his face. She pulled him close and kissed him again. She didn't have the words to tell him how much it meant to her that he wanted her to be his first, so she tried to tell him with the kiss.

As they kissed she rolled him onto his back. She pushed her hips into his hips, sliding her wet and open body over his erection. The tip of his penis nudged the entrance of her vagina. Without breaking the kiss she pushed back. As wet as she was, the tip slid right in. Julien raised his hips and inch by inch he entered her completely.

Remi placed her hands on either side of Julien's shoulders and pulled back from this kiss. His eyes were closed, his lips slightly parted. She pushed against him again and his shoulders rolled off the bed.

"Remi," he panted. She'd never loved the sound of her name so much as when he said it.

"Hold my hips," she whispered, not wanting to break the spell of the moment.

He took her hips in his large strong hands and held them tight as she moved on him. She kept the pace slow and easy, letting Julien get used to being inside a woman before taking things further. Looking down, she saw where their bodies united and became one. Julien was looking too.

She took a deep breath. She would start slow with him, let him feel everything as she moved on him. Remi tried not to go over the edge herself as she rode him with each sway of her hips, each undulation. His hands held her thighs, and she let him set the pace of her movements at first, the rhythm of their joining.

Joining…that was it. She couldn't think of what they did in this bed together as fucking, although she knew that was what the world would call it. She'd fucked him with her eyes the moment she'd seen him again for the first time in four years standing in his doorway. He'd fucked her with his fingers moments ago as she'd lay splayed open for him against his pillows. He'd fucked her with his mouth, and now she fucked him for the first time in his short life, which could have been so much shorter—a thought that terrified her. But this didn't feel like fucking to her, even as the room grew warm from their bodies and sweat trickled down her back and his fingers smelled of her arousal and his mouth tasted of her desire. She licked it off his lips.

For four years their two families had pushed apart from each other—a foolish, drunken quarrel that forced everyone to pick a side and go to war. But here on these pale gold sheets where Julien Brite's body disappeared inside Remi Montgomery, the rift they'd accidentally caused one foolish night mended inside her.

Remi pressed her palms onto Julien's chest and drove her pelvis into his with concentrated effort, clenching her inner muscles tightly around him. She wanted him to feel everything as she rode him. His back bowed underneath her, his length deep in her, hot and hard. She ground into him, against him, on him, with a renewed frenzy while beneath her Julien gasped and breathed and gasped again. He'd lost control of himself and nothing could stop him from lifting his hips in short, hard pulses as if seeking to tunnel as far into Remi as possible.

Their bodies were slick with sweat. She could hear the wetness that sealed him to her with each movement. The heat grew almost unbearable. She felt light-headed even as a heaviness settled into her lower body. Julien latched onto her right breast and sucked her nipple with desperate hunger. They had promised tonight last names would be banished. She was Just-Remi and he Just-Julien. But in that moment when he was inside her, they couldn't possibly have been more joined to each other. Even their first names disappeared and they became nothing but a man and a woman driving their needs into each other, taking their pleasure from each other and surrendering their lives to each other.

Julien's head fell back onto his pillow, his lower back arching off the bed as he came inside her, filling her up, coating the walls that clasped him. As he came, Remi rode him into the bed with wild movements that brought her to the edge and left her hanging there. Julien emerged from his haze long enough to press two fingers into her clitoris so deep they almost slid inside her. The touch, rough but necessary, sent her falling over the edge. She collapsed onto his chest as her second climax shook her to the core.

Haltingly and carefully, they disentangled from each other. A pure, pervasive exhaustion suffused her entire being. She could do nothing but roll onto her back and let the night air cool her burning skin. Julien's wetness poured out of her, glazing her thighs and staining the sheets. She did the math and realized it was nearly six in the morning back in Kentucky. She wanted to stay up all night with Julien, but her body wouldn't let her. Tomorrow they would do this again and again and again.

Remi waited for Julien to speak, to laugh or sigh or to

congratulate himself in some way for divesting himself of his virginity, and with an older woman, too. It was what she'd expect from any young man who'd fought long and hard to live long enough to experience a night like tonight. But he wasn't just any young man.

"You are the only person on earth my parents would hate for me to get involved with. Man. Woman. They don't care as long as I'm happy and he or she isn't you. And it's you," Julien said with a rueful laugh. "We're going to get in huge trouble for this, aren't we?"

In this torrid hour when he should have been thinking of sex and passion and conquest and everything that had happened and would no doubt happen again between them, instead he thought of her, of them, of what the future held, and what price they'd be asked to pay for what they'd done. Their families were very likely making a lot of money for stoking a very ugly rivalry in the press, and with one act, Remi and Julien had just merged the two families.

"With who?" she asked.

"Our—" he began and stopped. She heard his laugh, felt the bed move with it, then felt the bed move again as he lay on his side and rested his hand on her still quivering stomach.

"No one," he said. "No one at all."

CHAPTER SIX

A Fool's Paradise

Remi awoke with the first light and found Julien already up and sitting by the window. He had something in his hands—a book or magazine. She couldn't tell. She looked at him sitting in the sunlight. In the glint of the morning she could see every inch of the long pink scar on his chest. Nothing scared Remi—not spiders, not snakes, not jumping horses. But the idea that she'd almost lost Julien before she'd found him again—that terrified her. She said a silent prayer of thanks he'd survived his battle with cancer, which made this morning and every other morning she planned to wake up with him possible.

"Morning already?" she asked, pulling the covers over her breasts and sitting up.

"Unfortunately," he said. In nothing but a pair of pale blue boxers, he walked over to the bed and leaned in for a kiss. "Good morning."

"Morning breath," she warned.

"Don't care," he said and kissed her hard and deep before pulling back and smiling at her. "I woke up without my stu-

pid virginity hanging over my head. You think a little morning breath is going to bother me?"

"Your virginity was hanging over your head?" Remi
asked. "And I thought hymens were weird."

Julien laughed and pulled her into his arms. Remi sighed,
deeply contented despite the lingering worry in the back of
her mind. She couldn't bear the thought of leaving Julien,
and yet she could stay in Paris only so long before everyone
back home got dangerously suspicious.

"Thank you for last night," he said, kissing her neck and
her shoulders.

"I should thank you. That was amazing," she said. "It
might have been your first time, but it was my best time."

"Best time? Are we talking sex or races?"

She laughed again. "Sorry. Hard to get my head out of
the business."

"You really run things at Arden, don't you?" Julien
stretched out next to her in bed. He slid his hand under the
sheets and rubbed her hips and thighs.

"I do. At least I thought I did before all this mess. Mom
and Dad have been running the show behind my back. I'm
more than a little pissed off about that."

"I don't blame you," he said. "I'm pretty pissed, too. I
don't know how bad this could get, but I know when there's
gambling and race fixing and professional sports involved,
it can be—"

"—a disaster," she completed for him. "Pete Rose banned
from baseball. Lance Armstrong stripped of his medals and
jerseys. Reggie Bush giving back the Heisman."

"You know so much more about sports than I do."

"You're not a typical guy, are you, Julien?" Remi asked.

"In the hospital, the nurses would hang out in my room
with me longer if I had soap operas on. And my sisters would

visit and that's what they wanted to watch. That and *Grey's Anatomy.* I put my foot down over that one. I had enough hospital drama in my own life."

Remi almost smiled, but she saw Julien wasn't joking.

"That must have been lonely," she said. "Being in the hospital all the time."

"Mom and Dad worked their asses off with the farm. My sisters were in school. I don't blame them. They loved me and visited me every chance they got. But still I was alone a lot. My brain was my best company."

Remi wrapped her legs around him.

"If I had known you were in the hospital by yourself, I would have visited you every day," she said and meant it. "I would have hung out with you and watched sports with you and made sure you never ever had to watch *General Hospital.* I don't care what my parents would have said about it, I would have been there for you."

"You were there for me. Sort of," he said, and Remi noticed a faint blush on his cheeks.

He got out of bed and walked to the window seat. When he came back to the bed he held a magazine in his hand.

"That's a *Horse and Hound* magazine, Julien," she said. "You are doing porn the wrong way. Let me get you a *Playboy* subscription, please. Or introduce you to the Internet."

Julien grinned and flipped through the worn and wrinkled pages. "Mom brought me her old magazines to read in the hospital. Remember this issue?"

Remi glanced at the cover. It did look familiar to her. "Yeah, I did dressage for years. I won a medal when I was twenty-two."

"And you and your team got a photo spread in here," Julien said. "Look at that."

He flipped to a page near the center of a magazine. "Who

is that smoking-hot chick in the riding clothes?" he asked, pointing at a smiling blonde girl in buckskin jodhpurs, a white shirt with a gold pin through her stock tie, a chocolate-colored coat, buff leather riding gloves and black riding boots. The young woman had her hair plaited in an elegant French braid and wore no makeup but tasteful pale pink lip-gloss.

"That would be me with the helmet hair."

"You look so hot in this picture that for two years every sexual fantasy I had involved a girl in a dressage uniform."

"Seriously?" Remi laughed.

"Dead serious."

"I'm not showing any skin in the pic," she said, remembering the days of sweltering under that coat. "Can't see anything but my face."

"It left everything to my very good imagination. Remi... those boots..."

"You like the leather boots, huh?" she asked, giggling like she was back in college again and had nothing on her mind but boys and horses.

"I had dreams about those boots." He practically growled the words.

"So when I showed up in your living room yesterday...?"

"I was pretty sad you weren't wearing the boots."

"I still own those boots," she whispered into his ear then bit his earlobe for good measure. Julien groaned softly. "I have so many pairs of boots."

"There are horses in France," he said, sliding on top of her. "In case you want to go riding."

"I did a little riding last night," she said.

Julien laughed and buried his head against her neck. "More than a little."

"You want to try this morning?" She relaxed underneath him.

"We can do it again?" he asked.

"All you want," she said, kissing him. "And maybe later… I'll wear the boots for you."

Julien was already so eager he didn't even take off his boxer shorts before pulling his erection through the slit and settling between her open thighs. Using her hands, Remi opened herself up for him. Julien penetrated her easily, as she was still wet from last night. She sighed with pleasure as she lifted her hips to take every inch of him.

His thrusts were slow this morning, tentative and unsure. She guessed he wanted to prolong the coupling and avoid coming too soon. He was young, new at sex and no doubt worried about embarrassing himself with his inexperience, and she adored him for it.

"Your cock feels incredible inside me." Remi ran her hands through his mussed morning hair. "In case you were wondering."

"I was," he said, his voice slightly strained.

"I love your body, too." Remi ran her hands up and down his back, so lean and smooth-skinned. "Everything about you turns me on."

"Everything?" he asked between kisses.

"Everything," she repeated, as he rose up and put his hands on either side of her shoulders. She opened her legs wider, cupping the back of her knees with her hands.

"You're trying to make me come, aren't you?" Julien closed his eyes tight.

"Oh, no. You're not allowed to come. Not yet."

"I almost died once, Remi. Are you trying to kill me again?"

"Only in the fun way," she said.

"The French do call the orgasm 'the little death.'"

"No dying for you," she said as he kept thrusting slowly into her. "Not until I tell you to."

"I want you to come, too. What do I do?"

Remi gave him a mischievous grin. "Keep doing that. And watch the show."

He sat on his knees and resumed his hard, steady thrusts. Remi slipped a hand between her legs and found her clitoris.

"Oh my God," he breathed.

"Just focus on what you're feeling," she said as she closed her eyes. "I'll focus on what I'm feeling."

"What are you feeling?"

"You inside me," she said, her eyes still closed. "The ridge on the head of your cock is really pronounced. I can feel it rubbing against some really nice places."

"Seriously?" He sounded equal parts pleased and fascinated.

"Seriously. And it's a really good feeling. When I get turned on I get really hot."

"You are hot."

She laughed again. "The other kind of hot. And my boobs feel huge. Do they look huge? When I have sex they feel massive."

Julien cupped both her breasts in his hands.

"They're the perfect size for my hands."

"Then don't let go. I love feeling your hands on my breasts."

"I'll never take them off," Julien pledged.

"Good."

"Remi?" He stopped thrusting for a moment, and the pause in the pleasure wrenched her back to reality.

"Something wrong?" she asked.

"No. Maybe. I'm falling in love with you. Is that bad?"

Remi raised her arms and Julien fell into them.

"No," she said. "It's crazy. It's stupid. It's irrational and probably dangerous. But it's not bad. And I think I'm falling in love with you, too. It scares the hell out of me, but it's not going to go away anytime soon, so we might as well enjoy it."

"Like this?" he said, with a thrust that Remi felt in the pit of her stomach.

"Exactly like that."

He kneaded her breasts as he rode her with long thrusts. As Remi rubbed her pulsing clitoris, Julien pinched her nipples and squeezed her breasts. Ecstasy washed over and through her as Julien pounded into her. Little cries echoed from the back of his throat, barely restrained moans.

She raised her hand to his face and caressed his lips. He opened his eyes and looked down into hers.

"Come," she said. "Inside me."

His head lifted slightly, his hands gripped her hard, and he came with a quiet gasp in the back of his throat.

Remi was so close to coming...so close. Julien pulled out of her but soon he replaced his penis with his fingers. He ground three fingers into her wet opening, thrusting hard into her just the way she liked it. Julien licked and sucked her hard and swollen nipples as she arched into his mouth.

Had she ever felt anything this good before? Anything this right? Anything this sensual and hot and wrong and right all at the same time? There was no part of her body that didn't burn with desire right now. She'd never felt this sexual, this desired, this needed...and she never wanted it to end.

Her orgasm crashed through her so powerfully it almost hurt. Every nerve fired in her back and belly, and her clitoris throbbed against her fingers.

Spent at last, she rolled onto her stomach. Julien threw a leg over her lower back as he kissed her shoulders.

"You know what the crazy thing is?" Remi said, still panting. "Sex gets better the more times you have it."

"If it gets any better, my dick is going to break off."

"We'll glue it back on. We've got a whole farm full of horses we can—"

"Boss?" Merrick's voice came through the door, and the entire room rattled with the force of his knocking.

"I'm kind of doing something here, Merrick," Remi said, rolling her eyes.

"I know you're done fucking. The dishes in the sink aren't rattling anymore. Thought it was a damn Parisian earthquake."

"Fine. We're done. What do you want?"

"I don't want anything except breakfast and a raise, but we'll talk about that later. You're wanted. You left your phone out here, and you have six missed calls from the farm."

"It's Sunday," she groaned.

"Tell that to the fucking horses," Merrick said.

"I'll be right out," she said.

"Put on clothes first," Merrick ordered. "And take a shower."

"Anything else, Mr. Feingold?"

"Brush your teeth. And tell Julien to get dressed, too. We need to figure our shit out."

"We have shit to figure out?" she asked.

"What's your last name?" Merrick demanded through the door.

"Montgomery."

"What's the last name of the guy you've been banging all night?"

"Point taken," she said with a sigh. "I'll be out in half an hour. Take the credit card and go get us some...I don't know. Croissants? That's what French people each for breakfast, right?"

"Way to buy into a cultural stereotype, Boss," Merrick said.

"Actually they do eat croissants for breakfast," Julien said.

"I'm not talking to you, Julien Brite," Merrick said, sounding highly perturbed. "I bite my thumb at you. You sullied my lady's virtue. And if you're anything like me, you sullied her chest and her face, too."

"But it was really good sullying," Remi yelled back. "Really *really* good sullying."

"Oh," Merrick said. "Party like a cock star, then. Breakfast in thirty."

Remi showered and brushed her teeth with a new toothbrush Salena had left for her. She then wrapped her wet hair into a loose bun and pulled on yesterday's clothes. The entire time she rehearsed the speech she would have to give her father about where she'd disappeared to and why she hadn't answered her phone. She was a terrible liar, especially to her parents. She was nineteen before she lost her virginity, because she couldn't bear to lie to her parents about what she'd done on her dates. She'd had to wait until college. If they caught her with Julien Brite, plotting against both families, it would be a tragedy of Shakespearean proportions.

"Croissant?" Merrick tossed a bag at her as she emerged into the living room.

"Delivery. Nice," she said, digging into the bag. Merrick sat in a large dark green armchair with Salena on his lap. He was feeding her bites of croissant.

"Do you believe in hole 'n' stick medicine?" Merrick asked Salena.

"Holistic medicine?"

"No, this is a different thing."

Remi coughed loudly to get Merrick's attention.

"She must need more hole 'n' stick medicine," Merrick stage-whispered to Salena.

"Merrick," Remi said and snapped her fingers. "You yelled at me to get out of the most comfortable bed I've ever slept in with the sexiest, most amazing guy I've ever met. Focus, please. What's the situation?"

"Seven missed calls now," Merrick said. "Dad. Mom. Trainer. Mom. Dad. Trainer. Last one from your mother."

"Oh God, not my mother," she groaned and collapsed onto the sofa. Julien emerged from his bedroom, fully dressed and looking adorably sheepish. Salena grinned at him, and he turned a becoming shade of scarlet.

"What's going on?" Julien asked, sitting next to Remi on the sofa.

"Trying to figure out what to tell my parents about where I am. I can't say I'm on vacation. That's too suspicious. I'm not the whirlwind-vacation-taking type. At least I wasn't," Remi said.

"You." Merrick pointed at her. "You aren't going to say anything to them. You're a terrible liar. Just tell me when we're going back to Kentucky, and I'll handle it. When are we going back?"

Remi shrugged. "I don't know. We can't stay here long."

"Yes, you can," Julien said, giving her an almost pleading look. "At least stay as long as you can."

"Brilliant idea," Merrick said, rolling his eyes. "I'll just run out and get us two French citizenships and a bag of money so we don't have to go back to our jobs, and we'll move right in and eat croissants and fuck all the time. Wait. That's actually an amazing idea."

"Sounds good to me," Salena said, winking at him.

"We can't stay," Remi said, smiling apologetically at Julien. It hurt to say the words, but it was better to say them now, get them out, and deal with the fact of them. "I have a job. So does Merrick. And while I might be furious at my parents for whatever they're into, I can't abandon the farm. I love the horses too much."

"You really love it there?" Julien asked.

"I do," she sighed. "I did. I liked being in charge. I liked being responsible for the well-being of the horses and the jockeys. I take really good care of them." She was speaking in the past tense and it scared her. Something told her that her days as Arden Farm's manager were numbered.

"She does," Merrick said. "Arden Farms has the lowest horse and jockey injury record of any Thoroughbred horse farm in the U.S."

She shook her head and exhaled through her teeth.

"All this work I do," she said, standing up. "Every safety measure we've implemented, all the progress we've made...if my family gets caught by the racing commission fixing races or taking kickbacks from the track? It's all gone."

"I won't let them fuck over your work, Boss," Merrick said.

Remi smiled at him, something she rarely did. "When I was a kid, I went to Keeneland Racecourse with my dad for the horse auctions. And he told me that in the 1950s, Keeneland paid for every preschooler in Lexington, Kentucky, to get the polio vaccine. He told me that and I said then and there, that's what Arden Farms would be like. We would give back to Kentucky like that. And now..."

It broke her heart to even think of it, to think of all her hard work being tarnished by a scandal she had nothing to do with. She couldn't bear to face it. Eventually she would have to face it.

"Tell my father we're in New York," she said. "Tell him we'll be back by next weekend."

"Next weekend?" Julien sounded devastated.

"I have to work," she said. "I have responsibilities. I have to take care of the farm before my family makes everything fubar."

"Fubar?" Salena repeated.

"Fucked Up Beyond All Recognition," Merrick translated.

"Lovely," Salena said. "So where—"

The buzzing of Remi's phone silenced the entire room.

Remi took a deep breath. Merrick held out his hand. Remi winced and handed him the phone.

"Merrick here," he answered. Remi grabbed Julien's hand for comfort. She couldn't bear to look so she put a hand over her eyes.

"Remi? She's still out," Merrick said to whoever had called—her father, most likely. "I know. She misplaced her phone. We just found it. Women. Am I right?"

Remi heaved a sigh of relief. Having such a bizarre assistant paid off sometimes.

"Where's Remi? She's out in the stables with this guy…I don't know his name. She got a hot tip on a couple horses."

Good, Remi thought. Dad loved it when she aggressively went after a good horse.

"What horses?" Merrick repeated. "I don't know. Brown ones?"

Remi tried to grab the phone from Merrick. He slapped her hand away.

"Any luck with the horses?" Merrick repeated. "Yeah, she's found herself a nice young colt. She rode him last night."

Remi slapped a hand over her mouth to stop her from yelling at Merrick.

"How big is the colt?" Merrick said. "That's kind of a personal question. Big enough to enjoy the ride, not so big she can't walk today, I guess."

Remi glanced at Julien through a slit between her fingers. He'd fallen onto his side on the sofa and lay curled in the fetal position with a pillow smashed on his face. He was either laughing or crying. She couldn't quite tell which.

"Yeah, I'll have her try to call you once she's back in," Merrick continued. "We're getting shitty reception out here in the country, so don't freak out if she doesn't call you back right away. We'll be back this weekend."

Merrick ended the call and tossed Remi the phone. "You're good," he said. "I covered your ass."

"You told my father I rode a fine young colt last night," she nearly screamed.

"What? You did," he said.

"He had a point," Julien said, waggling his eyebrows. He lay back on the couch, his ankles crossed on the armrest. All she wanted to do was drag him back to bed with her. But instead she had to think, to plan.

"Come on," she said to Julien as she reached out her hand to him. He took it and she started to pull him to his feet. "I only have a few days left with you before I have to go back. Show me Paris."

"No," Julien said.

"No? You're not going to show me Paris?" Did he really think they could spend the next few days fucking? Well, if he wanted to try, she was game.

"I will show you Paris, yes. But you aren't going back."

"Julien, I told you. I have a job. A very important one and—"

"*We* are going back," Julien said. "All four of us. Right, Salena?"

Salena smiled at Julien. "I go where you go," she said to him, a display of loyalty that made Remi love Salena just a little bit. What next? Was she going to love Merrick?

"And I come where you come," Merrick said to Salena and bopped her on the tip of her nose. Nope. No love for Merrick.

"It's settled then," Julien said.

"You're coming back with me?" Remi asked, her heart fluttering with the new and dangerous love she felt for Julien.

"Yes. I just got you back. I'm not going to let you go that easily this time," Julien said, taking both her hands in his.

"Julien, I don't want to leave, either, but we can't be seen together. And I don't want to drag you into this mess. I can take care of it on my own. Merrick and I can, and then we'll come back here."

"I don't care if you can take care of it on your own," he said. "You're not on your own. It's my family's mess, too. I don't know what the plan is but I don't care. I'm going. We're in this together."

She sighed and then smiled. "Okay, we're in this together," she agreed. "Whatever this is. We need a plan."

"I've got the plan," Merrick said. "First I get hard evidence that both families are involved in whatever they're involved in. Then we put the thumbscrews on your parents."

"How do you propose to get hard evidence?" Remi asked him.

"The usual," Merrick said. "I'll sneak into the offices and snoop. Hopefully I won't find naked pics of your mom. Again."

"Nice plan, but someone's always at our house," Remi reminded him. "And my family doesn't like you or trust you."

"That's entirely fair," Merrick conceded. "What about you, Ginger?"

"My dad has an office at the house, too," Julien said. "I can try to dig around at night."

"Do you have any idea what you're looking for?" Merrick sounded skeptical.

"Well…no," Julien admitted.

"You know anything about gambling?" Merrick asked. "Anything about business, finance, or record keeping?"

"No."

"Are you a computer hacker and/or know your parents' passwords to their bank accounts so you can see if you they perhaps have received payments from mysterious sources?"

Julien sighed. "Okay, you got me there."

"Then I have to do it," Merrick said. "I just have to get into your house. Is it alarmed?"

"Not when we're home."

"Cool. We'll need to get everyone in your house out of your house—at night, preferably—and we have to make sure they're in such a tizzy—"

"A tizzy?" Remi repeated.

"A stone-cold motherfucking tizzy," Merrick said. "They need to be gone for several hours with no chance of them returning and walking in on me à la the Christmas party four years ago. I hack naked. It's just a thing. Don't ask."

"Then what's the plan?" Remi asked. "You have one, yes?"

"Yeah, and it's a fucking good one," Merrick said. "It's also insane and horrible and you're probably not going to go for it."

"Let us decide that," Remi said, although she truly dreaded whatever was about to come out of Merrick's mouth. If even he thought the plan was insane and horrible, she could only imagine her reaction to it.

"I'm not telling," Merrick said.

"Why not?" Remi narrowed her eyes at him. Of all times to be abstruse.

"Because you'll kill me," Merrick said, wincing. "I'll be worm food."

"Stop being a drama queen and tell us the damn plan,"

Julien said. Remi heard a note of command in his voice and liked it. He might be young but he wasn't weak.

Merrick raised his hands in surrender. "Fine. Stop pressuring me. I feel violated," he said. "So...the plan."

"Yes...?" Remi waved her hand to encourage further words.

"First, we're going to need a priest."

CHAPTER SEVEN

Santa Claus and the Banana

A week in Paris with Julien was one perfect moment after another for Remi.

Perfect Moment #1—Julien dipped her and kissed her under the Arc de Triomphe, which led to a crowd of tourists applauding them.

Perfect Moment #2—Julien took her to the Musée de l'Orangerie, where they stood in silence holding hands as they stared into the deep blue of Monet's *Water Lilies*. They didn't say a word in the room. Words would have been an insult to the lilies. Remi realized that day she enjoyed being silent with Julien as much as she enjoyed their conversations. She'd never been able to say that about anyone else before.

Perfect Moment #3—All four of them—Remi and Julien, Merrick and Salena—spent hours and euros galore in Shakespeare and Company. They bought more books than they could possibly fit in their suitcases. Salena bought French novels. Julien bought history books. She bought a little bit of everything. And Merrick bought erotica. All of it. The entire section. When she lamented her books wouldn't fit into her suitcase, Julien told her to leave them at his place, since she would need reading material when she came back to Paris with him again.

Perfect Moment #4—Remi and Julien's last night together before she left Paris. While Julien was inside her he whispered things into her ear they never taught her in sophomore high school French class.

J'ai envie de toi.

I want you.

Fais-moi l'amour.

Make love to me.

Je veux passer la reste de ma vie avec toi. S'il te plâit?

I want to spend the rest of my life with you. Please?

To that Remi had only one answer—*"Oui."*

On Friday morning, Remi kissed Julien goodbye *un, deux, trois* times, and she and Merrick boarded their return flight. She was leaving the City of Light and Julien for the Horse Capital of the World and her parents. She did not consider this a fair trade. Julien and Salena would wait a few days before following them back to Kentucky to avoid unnecessary suspicion.

Remi and Merrick barely spoke on the flight back, but he held her hand for part of the trip—a much-needed show of support and comfort.

"This is crazy," she whispered to him as their plane finally glided over American soil.

"I know," he said, and gave her that broad, wicked grin that sent women either running to him or away from him at top speed. "And that's why it's going to work."

"I can't believe I got—"

"Don't stress," Merrick said, squeezing her fingers. "Just tell yourself it's not real. That helps. Now, deep breaths. Focus. Eyes on the prize. We got this."

"The pep talk is not helping," she said.

"How about a finger bang?"

Remi glared at him.

"Don't say I never tried to help you," he said, shoving his sunglasses down on his face.

Remi pulled his sunglasses off his face and Merrick met her eyes.

"Julien was diagnosed with leukemia two weeks after we met," she said. "That's why he disappeared. Did Salena tell you?"

"Doctor-patient confidentiality," Merrick said, giving her a look of compassionate sympathy. "I had a hunch, though, when she told me she was an oncologist. I'm sorry he went through that. He's a good guy, good enough for you, and that's saying something."

"You know I hate you sometimes, right?" she asked, taking his hand.

"I'd be disappointed if you didn't."

"I do love you a little teeny tiny bit, too."

"Gross, Boss." He pulled his hand away from hers. "Don't make me call HR on you, you perv."

He gave her a wink and put his sunglasses back on. Then he patted his shoulder. Remi rested her head against him and slept there until they landed.

She did her best to play it cool when they returned to their normal schedule. Luckily her father was too busy to interrogate her about the unplanned horse-hunting trip she'd taken, seemingly on a whim. The irony of it was that he trusted her implicitly, and she no longer trusted her father at all.

She tried to concentrate on her work that week—scheduling races, meeting trainers—but Julien had taken over her mind. She thought of his face, so angular and striking. She thought of his skin—so young and smooth and warm. She thought of his body and how it belonged on top of her, inside her, underneath her, and every other sexy position she could think of. She missed the light citrus smell of his sheets on her skin and his arms that had held her as she'd fallen asleep during the all-too-brief nights she'd spent in his bed.

On her way to her small house that sat on the edge of her parents' thousand-acre property, Remi's phone buzzed with a text message.

Here, the message read. Remi grinned at her phone. Finally she and Julien were on the same continent again.

Where? she wrote Julien back, desperate to see him.

My family picked us up at the airport, he wrote. Trapped with them. That's why I'm texting instead of calling.

Remi stared at her phone as she unlocked her door and walked into her house. She'd lived in it for three years, and it had never felt empty or lonely to her. But now it needed something, someone else here. That someone else was unfortunately trapped at his parents' house.

I need to see you, came the next message from Julien. Five little words that made Remi's heart dance, her stomach trip, and her feet flutter.

Tell me when and where and I'll be there, she wrote back.

Mom won't let me out of her sight for a couple days. We're visiting my grandparents in Ohio. I'm being smothered. I had cancer. Haven't I been through enough?

Your fault you're so damn cute.

I love you, came Julien's reply.

That too, she replied and then added an I love you of her own. She wasn't used to writing those words, saying those words, feeling those words. But the more she wrote them, spoke them, felt them, the better they fit onto her fingers, her tongue, her heart.

She went to bed alone and cursed the cold sheets. She had loved sleeping with Julien. Every night after sex, he'd rubbed her back while they'd talked. Their very last night together had been their best night. They'd dared to discuss the future, a future they could share. Remi had asked Julien what he wanted to do with his life.

"I never thought about the future before I had leukemia," he'd answered, as Remi curled up on his chest. She'd gotten so used to his scar by now she rested her head over it without a second thought. "So maybe one good thing came out of being sick. Now I know what I want to do with my life."

"Which is?"

"Help teenagers with life-threatening illnesses. I don't want to be a doctor. That's not my thing. I want to help them the way Salena helped me—by getting me out of the house. I don't know what to do with that dream yet, but at least I have one now. You? Do you always want to work at Arden?"

"Not anymore," she'd confessed. "The place seems tainted now by what my parents are up to. I still want to work with horses, but I want to find a way to be around horses and do something with them other than running them into the ground. The best part of my job is the charity work we do at Arden, the people we help. I just want to find a way to do that as a full-time job."

"You dream good dreams," Julien said, kissing her on the top of the head.

"You're my best dream." They'd made love again after that and fell asleep tangled in each other. Five nights ago was the last time they'd been together. Five nights and an eternity.

She wouldn't survive another five nights and she told Merrick exactly that when he shuffled into work an hour late the next day with a big smile on his face.

"Did you spend the night at Salena's?" she demanded.

"Yup."

"You're fired."

"For getting laid?"

"Yes."

"My, aren't we sexually frustrated this morning," Merrick said, handing over her coffee.

"Five days," she said. "I'm not going to make it."

"You'll make it. If I can last five days you can last five days."

"Have you ever gone five whole days without sex?"

"Sure. Of course. Oh, you mean five *consecutive* days?"

"It's ridiculous. This isn't medieval England or Renaissance Italy. Families shouldn't be feuding."

"Tell that to Steve Harvey." Merrick said, sitting on her desk in front of her. "It must be awful for you. Julien's forbidden fruit. Taboo. Off the menu. *Verboten*. The scandal? The lies? The sneaking around? Terrible."

"Awful," Remi said.

"Horrible."

"Shameful."

"It's hot, isn't it?" Merrick asked.

"So fucking hot." Remi dropped her head to her desk and groaned. Merrick, knowing what was good for him, didn't laugh at her. Not too much anyway.

Remi knew she'd tear Julien's clothes off the second she saw him again, but when that would be she didn't know. Salena was still working out her end of the plan. Remi didn't want to rush things, but if she didn't see Julien again soon, she couldn't be held responsible for her actions. When she texted Merrick at midnight on Thursday, she knew she'd reached the end of her rope.

You awake? she wrote him.

No, I'm dead.

I'm thinking about the plan, she wrote him.

No, you aren't. You're thinking about fucking Julien. So just go fuck him and let me sleep, Merrick wrote. And then for some reason added emoticons of a grey alien, a skull, a bee, the flag of Japan, and seventeen eggplants. She should never have let him download the app on his work phone.

But it wasn't a terrible idea, sneaking over to Julien's for an hour or so. Well, no. It was a terrible idea and she knew it.

She wrote Merrick back.

What if I get caught at his house?

Merrick replied with a ghost and a Santa Claus.

WTF?

Be quiet as a ghost, he explained. Get in and out like Santa.

I was supposed to get that message from two emoticons?

Duh, he wrote back. Go get it.

And he punctuated his text with a rather phallic-looking banana emoticon, and that was logic that neither she nor her vagina could argue with. She threw on her clothes again and got into her car.

Capital Hills Farm constituted twelve hundred acres near Frankfort, the state capital. This late at night with no traffic to contend with, Remi made it to the farm gates in thirty minutes. She parked her car on a side road and carefully climbed over the white wooden fence.

"I can't believe I'm doing this," she whispered to herself as she crossed the dark, manicured lawn. Julien had said his family only alarmed the house when no one was at home. She hoped he was right about that. "How horny am I?"

Horny enough to risk a B&E conviction obviously.

"Julien, Julien…" she breathed, "where the hell are you, Julien?" The windows of the three-story colonial mansion were mostly darkened, but light glowed from two second-floor windows.

Did you get a fancy corner bedroom? she typed on her phone.

What? Julien replied. Yes. Why?

I'm looking at your window, she wrote back. If you love me, you won't call the cops on me.

She counted only two seconds before Julien's face appeared in the window. He opened his window and stuck his head out.

"You're crazy," he whispered. In the clear night air, the words carried right down to her. Her heart, already pounding from sneaking to his house, now leaped at the sight of him.

"Crazy for you. Will your mom let you come out and play?" She smiled up at him.

"It's fifty degrees out. You come in and play."

"Where?" she asked. She'd never been to the Brite family home before. He held up his finger in the universal sign of *Wait right there.*

Remi glanced around while she waited, hoping the Brites didn't have any rabid killer attack dogs wandering near the house tonight.

She heard a whistle and peeked around the corner of the

house. Julien stood on the back covered porch and waved her in. She ran to him and he caught her in his arms. In a frenzy of silent kisses, Julien pulled Remi into the house and shut the door behind them. He kissed her mouth, her neck, her earlobes and her throat while she ran her hands all over his bare chest. He must have been getting ready for bed, because his shirt and the top button of his jeans were already unbuttoned. Good. Less work for her.

"I missed you so much," Julien murmured as he nuzzled her hair.

"I shouldn't have come, but I couldn't wait anymore."

"It was killing me, too," Julien said, his hands sliding under the back of her shirt. He unhooked her bra and pulled her even tighter to him.

In the dark she could barely make out what room they were in, but it seemed to be a large office or a small library. Didn't matter what it was. They were alone, and that was all she cared about.

Julien dragged her skirt up to her stomach. Blood pounded through her. Her thighs felt tight and her stomach knotted itself up as Julien slid his hand into her underwear.

He found her clitoris with his fingertip and rubbed the swollen knot until she had to bury her mouth against his shoulder to keep from moaning audibly. She dug her nails into his back, holding on to him with everything she had. She shuddered hard in his arms when he pushed two fingers up and into her. Wet as she was, he slid right into her.

"I won't make it to my room." Julien rasped the words into her ear.

"Then just do it here."

Julien was fantastically good at taking orders—one good quality among many. He wrenched her panties down her legs and turned her back to him. During their nights in his

Paris apartment, she'd done everything she could to help him make up for all the time lost while he was sick as a teenage boy. She let him try any sexual position he wanted. Quickly they discovered together that Julien loved entering her from behind. She loved it, too, but at this point she wanted him so much she'd strap them both to roof of a moving car if that was the only way she could get it.

"What if your parents walk in on us again?" she teased. She heard Julien behind her unzipping his jeans.

"I locked the office door."

"What if they break in?"

"I'll tell them to wait their fucking turn, then."

He pulled her skirt up again and pushed his fingers into her. Remi arched her back and braced herself against the wall as he opened her up. Behind her Julien guided himself to her entrance. She pushed back and she felt the head bumping her G-spot. Remi sighed with the sheer relief of feeling Julien inside her again. She arched her back even more to take all of him inside her. He bottomed out and started thrusting. This was exactly what she needed.

"I can't get enough of you," Julien whispered as he pulled out all the way to the tip and crashed back into her. She forced herself to stay silent as he emptied her and filled her with each thrust. He slid his hands under her shirt and cupped her breasts. All Remi could do was hold herself still against the wall as Julien slammed into her again and again, the sounds of her wetness and his labored breathing accompanying his every move.

Her climax built quickly and she came hard, her inner muscles fluttering and clenching tightly around Julien's still thrusting length.

She went limp in his arms, and he pulled out of her. He turned her to face him and she wrapped her arms around his neck. He kissed her again, delving into her mouth with his tongue. He was backing her up as he kissed her. She didn't know and she didn't care where he was taking her, as long as he was taking her.

Something hit the back of her legs, and Julien lowered her down onto a leather sofa. He yanked her shirt up to expose her breasts and sucked hard on her nipples. He hadn't come yet and she wanted him to, needed him to. For six beautiful nights she'd fallen asleep with his semen in her and on her, a privilege she'd never granted any man before. They didn't use condoms simply because he'd been a virgin and was sterile. She'd known the moment she saw him that she wanted to give him everything she had and keep nothing from him.

Julien kissed his way down her stomach.

"Julien—"

"I have to taste you," he said. He held her by the backs of her thighs, and Remi obediently opened her legs for him. If he had to, he had to. Who was she to argue?

He licked the seam of her vulva from base to apex and down again. The leather couch creaked under them as he devoured her with deep and hungry kisses. He pushed his tongue all the way into her before focusing his attention solely on her clitoris. He licked it gently, sucked it greedily, and rubbed it until Remi couldn't stop herself from coming again, even harder this time. Her hips rose a foot off the sofa and as she came in dead silence, every part of her vibrating with pleasure.

She collapsed in a daze. Julien pushed between her legs again and entered her fast and hard. He went wild on top of her, fucking her as if he'd die if he stopped. Spent and drained, she could do nothing but lie beneath him and take his every rough and hungry thrust. She watched his face, studying the beauty of it. His eyes were closed to concentrate better on his pleasure, and his dark eyelashes fluttered on his cheeks. His face was flushed with desire, and his skin had pinked like a rose. Quiet breaths escaped through his slightly parted lips, and a swath of his unruly dark red hair fell over his forehead. He'd told her that he'd grown his hair out as soon as he could in a victory lap against the leukemia that had robbed him of it. She'd promised she'd never make him cut his hair as long as they lived if he didn't want to.

Reaching up, Remi swiped the lock of hair off his forehead and grazed his cheek gently with the back of her hand. His eyes flew open and he gazed down at her. He bore down on her and with his eyes locked on hers, came inside her

She smiled at him when the last of their frenzy had died down.

"I love you," he panted. "I keep thinking I'll get to the bottom of what I feel for you. And then I do and the bottom's just a lid and I open the lid and there's more love inside it. Was that stupid? I can't tell if it's stupid or poetic."

"It's perfect. And I feel the same way," she said, taking him in her arms. She felt his heart beating wildly against her own chest.

"I guess that's a good thing," he said. "Considering." He laughed, and the laughter shook her body and his.

"Exactly," she said. "Merrick is crazy. This plan of his is crazy."

"But it's going to work, right?" Julien asked.

"We'll make it work."

Julien pulled out of her and winced.

"Are you hurt?" she asked.

"No…just wet. And the couch is leather. And Mom sits here all the time."

"Oh no."

"Don't move," he said.

Don't move? Of course she wouldn't move. She clamped her thighs tight and waited for Julien. He came back with a box of tissues, and helped her with the cleanup. Two tissues for him, two for her, two for the couch.

"Six tissues," he said. "Wow."

"Some of that's mine," she said. "Still impressive, right?"

"New record for us."

They high-fived.

"You've been saving that up for a while, haven't you?"

"I was very close to taking matters into my own hands. Thank God you showed up and saved me from myself."

"I knew there was a reason I did something this stupid. It was all for you," she said, as Julien balled up the tissues. She got up and found her abandoned underwear and pulled them on while Julien opened a side door. She heard a toilet flushing. Good. Smart way to dispose of the evidence.

"I should go," she whispered, as he came back to her with his jeans now zipped and his hair somewhat tamed.

"No way. Not yet," he said.

"We can't get caught. And we're already pushing our luck here."

"My parents sleep like the dead. Stay for a little while, please."

"Will you show me your room?" she asked, grinning at him through the dark.

"Upstairs. Now," he said, and he grabbed her by the wrist. Luckily most of the house was carpeted, so they made almost no sound as they raced upstairs to Julien's room. When they reached his room she had to cover her mouth to stop herself from laughing uproariously. Julien's bedroom was a time machine. It was as if the year 2009 had been isolated and preserved in this one bedroom. A *Zombieland* poster hung on the wall. A poster for *The Dark Knight* hung next to it. A large CD player and two-foot-high speakers sat on a table. She hadn't owned a stereo system that large in years. An Eminem CD and a Lil Wayne CD sat side by side on top of the stereo.

"Wow," she breathed. "Am I in the past?"

Julien locked his bedroom door behind them. "Sort of."

"I like it. But then again, I had a big Christian Bale crush back then." She nodded at a *Dark Knight* poster. "You know, way back then. Not anymore."

"Such a girl," he said, rolling his eyes. "It's about Batman's toys. And that he doesn't use guns. Or kill people."

"And Christian Bale."

"Girl."

"Boy," she said. "Did your mom keep your room like this as a shrine?"

Julien laughed and pulled her to his bed—a full-size bed, thankfully. She'd worried it would be a twin.

"No. I was just too sick to care what posters were on the walls. The house has ten other guest rooms, so Mom's in no hurry to redecorate. And now I've moved out, so who cares what's on the walls?"

"Have you thought about living with me?" she asked. "I mean, once we go through with this plan."

"At your house on your parents' land?" He sounded dubious.

"Actually, I have a better idea. Tell you when this is all over."

"I'd live on the streets with you, Remi."

"Don't worry. I'm foreseeing much nicer accommodations for us. So you'll move in?"

"I love you," Julien reminded her. "And we're in this together."

"I love you, too. And I promise, this is going to work. And no one will keep us apart ever again."

She kissed him so he would know she meant it. And she did mean it. This love had charged into her life kicking up clods of dirt with fierce and flying feet. She'd never expected it, never saw it coming, never knew what hit her. She'd been run over by a team of wild horses and she couldn't have been happier about it.

"You know," Julien said into her lips, "I always wanted to have sex in my own bed at home while my parents were sleeping."

"You rebel."

"Want to?" he asked, pushing her onto her back again.

"Oh no, anything but that," she said, throwing her leg over his back.

Julien slid on top of her and the bedspring creaked loudly.

Someone knocked on his door.

Remi froze, her heart racing. She looked around wildly trying to find somewhere to hide.

Julien only rolled his eyes.

"Great timing," he sighed and stood up.

"What are you doing?" she rasped.

He smiled at her. "Showtime."

He opened the door, and Salena stepped inside his room. She had a cup of ice in her hand.

"Am I interrupting?" she asked, one elegant eyebrow arched at the both of them.

"We're done," Remi said.

"We weren't done," Julien said, "But I guess we are now."

"I got off the phone with my friend at the hospital," Salena said. "Now's the time. I called Merrick. He's ready. It's all ready."

Julien exhaled heavily and nodded. "Okay. Let's do this," he said.

"Open up. Time to lower your temperature." Salena popped an ice cube in his mouth and Julien sucked on it. "And you should go. This place will be crawling with people soon."

"We'll walk you out." Julien placed his hand on her lower back. "This probably shouldn't happen in here anyway, or they'll wonder why Salena was in my bedroom at one in the morning."

They returned to Julien's mother's office and Julien opened the door that led to the back porch. She wrapped one arm around his back and kissed him.

"No, no," Salena said, wagging her finger. "We want to lower his blood pressure, not raise it."

"Oops." Remi pulled back. With one private smile at Julien, she whispered, "It hurts to say goodbye to you. So I won't. I'll see you on the other side."

He kissed her forehead, and she left him and Salena alone in the office. The last thing she saw was Salena shoving a needle into Julien's arm and Julien collapsing onto the floor.

As she drove away from Capital Hills, two ambulances and a police car passed her. She knew exactly where they were going, and soon Merrick would be on his way here as well.

Julien and Salena were doing their part. Merrick would do his part soon. Only one thing left to do tomorrow morning.

Her turn.

CHAPTER EIGHT

Mr. and Mrs. Brite

At dawn, Remi got out of bed like usual, got dressed to go riding, and headed to the stables. Arden Farms was so large that workers drove golf carts between the stables, but she preferred to ride one of the working horses—usually one of their Tennessee walkers. This morning, however, she picked Benvolio. There wasn't a horse on the property that could jump like Benvolio could. Perfect.

"Don't be mad at me," she whispered to Benvolio as she tightened the girth. "I'm going to do something very stupid, but I won't let anyone blame you."

She fed Benvolio an apple and stroked his long nose. "You won't get turned into glue for this, I promise," she said, brushing a tangle out of his mane. "I'm crazy in love with someone and you're going to love him too when you meet him. So just trust me, okay?"

Benvolio didn't answer with anything but a nuzzle against her shoulder. She took that as a sign she had him on her side.

She stepped into the stirrup and swung her leg over his back. With a twitch of the reins he started down the path toward the practice track. She warmed Benvolio up with a few cross-rail jumps. Good. They could do this. As she neared the track she saw her father leaning against the fence like he had for as long as she could remember. Coffee cup in hand, newsboy cap covering his bald spot, and an intense look of concentration on his face as two of their strongest four-year-olds pounded down the practice track.

They passed the finish line, and she saw her father hit a button on his stopwatch. Finally he looked away from the track and noticed her. She waved at her father. He waved at her. And just as he was starting to look away again, Remi gave Benvolio the signal to break into a canter. She pointed him at a low fence, and he obediently jumped. Even though she knew she'd have one hell of a bruised ass from this little stunt, Remi let go of the reins in midair and fell from the saddle.

She hit the grass with a thud that rattled her teeth. Any other time she'd been knocked off a horse, she'd gotten right back up again. But not today. Today she was on a mission.

Instead of getting up, Remi closed her eyes.

Only seconds later she sensed herself being surrounded by people, nervous and scared. She heard her father's voice shouting for a doctor. She heard one of the trainers saying they should call 911 immediately. People called her name, patted her face, tried to pry open her eyelids.

Ten minutes later, she was in the back of a speeding ambulance. Her father had yelled he'd follow right behind in his car. As she was being loaded, she pretended to come to just long enough to ask her father to bring her mother, too. He promised he would.

Now it was on.

As soon as she was alone in the ambulance with the EMTs, she miraculously recovered and started talking. The EMTs said she'd be checked at the hospital for a concussion and monitored for a few hours. Of course she would. She knew exactly what would happen once she got to the hospital. In her twenty-six years she'd fallen off horses and bumped her head half a dozen times and had gone through this routine every time. She hated that she had to scare everyone like this, but she knew Merrick was right—this was the only way to guarantee both of her parents would be away from the farm long enough for him to do his digging. The guilty feeling gnawed at her, but considering her parents had involved the farm in possibly illegal activities, she decided giving their parents a brief scare was a fair trade for the hell they'd put her through.

Luckily, at the ER she was considered a low-priority patient as she was awake, alert, and seemingly unharmed. She was shunted into a side room and semiforgotten. Every fifteen minutes a nurse would peek in the door and make sure she was still conscious. The nurse asked if she wanted her parents back in the room. She politely declined the offer. Instead she turned on the television and found nothing on but soap operas.

So this is what Julien went through—sitting alone in a hospital room staring at a television and waiting for his life to start.

Finally, Merrick texted her.

Got it, was all the text said plus a rocket-ship emoticon.

Get here, she wrote back, and just because she loved him a little bit today, she added a smiley face.

And a banana.

Half an hour later, Merrick walked through her hospital room door. He had a file folder in his hand, two ledger books, and a sheaf of printed pages.

"Is that it?" she asked, as he sat on her bed and tossed the papers in her lap.

"All of it." He wore an ear-to-ear grin. The only thing that made Merrick happier than getting into trouble was getting someone else into trouble. "Read."

She read through everything he'd brought her—thinly veiled messages from Balt, payments recorded in her dad's old-school ledgers that weren't on the official set of books, and a damning e-mail from Julien's father to hers that implicated them all.

On the one hand she was thrilled they had hard evidence. On the other hand, she was more furious than ever.

"I'm going to kill them," she said once she'd finished reading.

"We're in a hospital. If you try to murder them, the doctors will just revive them," Merrick said.

"They might try to kill me," she said. "Probably good we're here."

"I won't let them, Boss. I'd kill for you, die for you, I'd even take a bare bodkin for you."

"You'd take a dagger for me?"

"I thought a bare bodkin was a penis."

"It's a knife."

"I've seriously been misreading the subtext of *Hamlet* then."

"Come on. We have two sets of parents to freak out."

She grabbed the pile of papers, and together they found her parents waiting in the lobby. Her father was on his phone, no doubt checking in with the farm. Her mother was flipping through a magazine without making eye contact with any of the pages.

"Good news," she said to them. "I'll live. No concussion."

"Oh thank God," her mother said, and reached out to hug her.

"You gave us a little scare there," her father said, stoic as always.

"I'm about to scare you two a little more," she said, refusing to return the hug. Merrick's find had implicated not just Julien's mother and father in this mess, but both her parents as well. "Merrick, what room is he in?"

"He's in 5515," he said.

"Who? What are you talking about, young lady?" her father asked, narrowing his eyes at her. "And is that my ledger book?"

Remi took a step back and crooked her fingers at her parents. "I have someone you two need to meet," she said. "I think you'll like him."

The elevator ride to the fifth floor was a bit awkward, but Remi refused to answer any of her parents' questions. "You'll see..." was all she said. On the fifth floor they walked past the nurses' station. A young nurse demanded to know whose room they were visiting.

Remi sighed. She was afraid this would happen. It was okay. She had this. "Julien Brite, room 5515."

"His parents have requested family only can visit."

Remi grabbed a sheet of paper off the nurse's station desk, then scrawled a few choice words onto the paper and handed it to the nurse.

"Oh," the nurse said. "Go right in."

"Thank you," Remi said.

"Remi Olivia Montgomery, you tell us right now what is happening," her mother demanded.

"Julien Brite?" her father repeated. "Young lady, didn't we tell you that you were never to see him again?"

"You did. I ignored you." Remi pushed open the door to room 5515. Julien was sitting up in bed surrounded by his family. She nearly cried at the sight of him in the hospital room. Hopefully this would be his last trip to a hospital for the rest of his life. Instead of crying, she kissed Julien.

"Excuse me, miss" came a woman's voice from behind her. Remi ignored it. She looked Julien in the eyes.

"Did we get it?" he whispered the question. He could have shouted it if he wanted to. Everyone in the room had recognized each other at once. Her parents began fighting with his parents. A nurse shouted over them all to shut them up. And in her peripheral vision she saw Merrick standing to the side and taking pictures of the melee and grinning.

"We got everything," she said and gave him one more long, lush kiss.

"Excuse me?" Remi felt a tapping on her back. She stood up, turned around and faced Mrs. Deidre Brite.

"Just what do you think you're doing?"

"I was just slipping the tongue to your son," Remi said with a smile.

"You were what?" she gasped.

"It's okay, Mom," Julien said. "Remi and I are sleeping together, so she's allowed to kiss me."

"Julien!" his father yelled.

"I'm going to need everyone to shut up and sit down right this second," Remi said. "Or stand. I don't care. But you all do need to shut the hell up, because Julien and I have a few very big announcements."

Julien hopped out of the hospital bed and stood at her side. Just then Salena in her white doctor's coat and blue scrubs entered the room and stood by Merrick. Good. They didn't want her to miss the show.

"Announcements?" her father said. "You drag us to a hospital to tell us you're dating Julien Brite? Remi, what the hell is going on here?"

"First of all, you should know Julien and I are fine. Neither one of us is sick or injured. We faked it to get you away from the farms so Merrick could do a little digging. He struck gold, in case you were wondering."

"Julien, you scared your mother and me to death—" Julien's father started, but Julien raised his hand, cutting him off.

"Yeah, well, you all scared me a little, too, by engaging in illegal activities. I think faking a faint is barely a misdemeanor, considering you all are committing felonies," Julien said.

"What are you talking about?" Mr. Brite demanded, his face red and angry.

"We'll get to that in a second," Remi said. "The second thing you need to know is that Julien and I are together. And that's the least of your problems."

"Problems?" Mrs. Brite repeated, looking nervously at her husband.

"Big problems," Julien said. "Remi, you know this stuff better than I do. Can you explain it?"

"Happily," she said. "You see, Tyson Balt owns Verona Downs. And Hijinks and Shenanigans are the favorites for the Verona Downs Stakes race. Everybody bets on the favorites. If they lose and one of the long shots wins, Tyson Balt and Verona Downs will be swimming in money. Mr. Balt paid our parents ten million dollars each to whip the press into a frenzy over the biggest horse-racing rivalry in decades and then throw the race. Neither Shenanigans nor Hijinks will win, and Balt will be richer than God."

Remi held up a sheaf of papers Merrick had printed out.

"Tyson Balt paid you all off to throw the Stakes race, and I have the proof right here. Don't even bother to deny it."

"Remi, honey," her mom began.

Remi held up her hand. "I don't want to hear any excuses,"

she said. "Do you know how much trouble you all could be in if the racing commission found out about this? Do you?"

All four parents remained silent.

"Do you have any idea how humiliating this would be if the scandal broke? It would be all over the racing news for weeks. Arden and Capital would become laughingstocks and pariahs. Pariahs," she repeated, knowing how much her family and Julien's cared about public opinion. "And all for what? Money."

"That money is your money, too," her father said. "We did this for you and the farm. Do you have any idea how expensive it is to run a Thoroughbred farm?"

"Of course I do," she said, pointing at herself. "I'm the damn farm manager, Dad. I know we're doing fine. We're not billionaires, but nobody's starving around here. And did you really think I wouldn't notice what asses you all were being in the news? That stupid feud should have never started to begin with. Julien and I got a little carried away, but it was nobody's business but ours. Did you think I would just stand by and let you all drag our good names through the mud? Did you think I wouldn't notice you bought the new farm and paid cash? Do you all think I wouldn't notice the Brites dropping ten million at the auctions? How stupid do you all think I am?"

She waited. No one wanted to touch that question. *Wise decision*, she thought.

"Here's the thing," Remi said as she took Julien's hand in hers. "I had my suspicions, and I needed someone in the Brite family to help me confirm them. Julien did. And in addition to helping us get all this lovely evidence, he and I... well, how would you put it?"

"We're in love," Julien said. "Madly and completely in love. For starters."

"What do you want with us?" Julien's stern father asked.

"That is a fantastic question," Remi said. "And luckily we have a fantastic answer. Capital Hills has a nice crop of yearlings. Arden just bought a second farm. You're going to give me and Julien the yearlings and the farm. We'll sell the yearlings and you all can call it a donation. Oh, and we want Shenanigans and Hijinks, too. You all don't deserve those horses." She would take Benvolio, too, since he was a coconspirator.

"You want what?" Mr. Brite asked, utterly aghast.

"A plague on both your horses!" Merrick shouted.

Remi turned around and glared at him.

"Sorry," he said. "I always wanted to say that."

"We want your ill-gotten gains," Julien said. "And we're going to use them for good. Remi and I are going to turn the farm into an equine therapy nonprofit to help sick, disabled and poor teenagers. And you all are funding it. Congrats. Criminals to philanthropists in one afternoon."

"We are, are we?" her father asked, sounding both angry and skeptical. "I'm not entirely sure I'm on board with this plan."

"Tough shit," Remi said. "You lost your vote in this matter when you put our entire farm and our family's reputation at risk. You all should be ashamed of yourselves. And even if you're not, you're going to make amends for it anyway."

"She's so sexy when she gets tough like this," Merrick said.

"Totally agree," Julien said, and he and Merrick fistbumped.

"The Brites and the Montgomerys can't simply start a nonprofit together," Mrs. Brite said. "We're incorporated businesses. And the rivalry in the press—"

"Is over," Remi said. "Done. Finished. Kaput. It's history. Now and forever. And you all will be holding a press conference in one week to announce to the world that the feud is over. The Brites and the Montgomerys have forgiven each other. The press will eat it up. Then you'll announce that the creation of Shenanigans—a day camp that will be funded by Arden Farms and Capital Hills for needy, sick and disabled teenagers. And you won't be taking another cent from Tyson Balt ever again. You won't be betting money on horse racing ever again. And you won't be throwing another race. Ever. Again."

Remi paused and let the words sink in.

"And if we don't?" Mr. Brite asked after a minute's pause.

"Your son and I will be giving the racing commission a call."

"You'd turn on us? Your own family?" her father asked.

"Me? *I'm* the one turning on the family?" Remi was aghast. "You got greedy and put our good name and reputation at stake. Julien and I could have just called the commission. Instead we're giving you all a way to exit this idiocy with grace and dignity."

"I don't even know who you are anymore. This isn't the Remi Olivia Montgomery I know and love," her mother said in her most scolding tone.

"No, it isn't," Remi said. "Because I'm not Remi Olivia Montgomery."

"What?" her mother gasped.

"She's Remi Olivia Brite," Julien said with a wide victorious smile. "We got married in Paris. Merrick took pictures."

"They're right here," Merrick said and held up his iPhone. "Doesn't Remi look pretty in her dress? I picked it out. Oh, and here's the marriage document-license-thingie." He held the certificate up for the room to see. "*Voila!* That's French for *'Voila!'*"

"It's a good thing we did get married," Remi said, turning to kiss him quick on the mouth. "The nurse said family only was allowed in your room. I wrote her a little note that said I'm your wife and these are your in-laws."

"Hi, in-laws," Julien waved at the room.

"You got married?" Mrs. Brite breathed, staring bug-eyed at her son.

"I know it's a little sudden," Julien admitted, wincing. "But it was the best way to guarantee…What did you call it, Merrick?"

"A merger," Merrick said. "And these two kids have been merging like crazy. In your house last night, even."

"I can't help it," Remi said without apology. "I missed my husband."

"My daughter and Julien Brite got married," her mother repeated. "Married? Married to Julien Brite?"

"Say 'married' a few more times," Merrick said. "It's starting to sound like 'Merrick.'"

"It was definitely a wedding. There was a French minister, and we were in a church and it was all quite romantic," Remi said, her voice strong and true. True because it was true—the church, the flowers, the ceremony. "Sorry you missed it."

Her mother looked at Remi, then Julien, then back at Remi, and sat back down in her chair. But she didn't faint, so that was good.

"Are you telling us the truth?" her father demanded. He stared her straight in the eyes.

Remi calmly faced her father. "Church. Minister. Wedding ceremony. Me. Julien. Vows. Document signed, sealed and…" She grabbed the document from Merrick's hand. "And delivered."

She gave the marriage certificate to her father.

"You're not lying," her mother said, looking wild-eyed at the document.

"Mom, you've been telling me for two years to find a nice guy and settle down. I found the nice guy. We're settling down. And yes, it is sudden and shocking, but it is also the smartest thing I've ever done."

"Can't wait for the honeymoon," Julien said.

"Will you marry me?" Merrick said to Salena.

"Absolutely not," Salena said.

"Is it because I'm Jewish and you're Hindu?"

"It's because you're bizarre, arrogant and insufferable."

Merrick didn't seem at all surprised or disappointed. "We can keep banging, though, right?"

"That goes without saying."

"You too, Salena?" Mrs. Brite demanded. "You're in on this too?"

"I am," Salena said. "Also, I quit."

"And I quit," Remi said.

"I do too," Merrick said.

"I don't have a job," Julien said. "But if I *did* have a job on the farm, I'd also quit it."

Remi's mother had her hand on her forehead. Her father looked like he might throw up. Julien's father and mother were arguing with each other. No one was having a heart attack.

She'd call it a win.

"Mom and Dad," Remi said after a deep breath, "I love you both. But what you did is almost unforgivable. You all should be ashamed of yourselves." She stared down every parent in the room. That none of them could meet her eyes was the final proof of their guilt. "Be as angry at us as you want right now. But we did this for your own good, and you'll see that eventually. Now if you'll excuse me, my husband and I are going on our honeymoon. Shall we, Mr. Brite?"

"I've made a miraculous recovery overnight, Mrs. Brite," Julien said. "You mentioned a honeymoon?"

"Any suggestions?" Remi asked.

Julien shoved his feet into his shoes and grabbed his jacket.

"I have an idea," Merrick said.

By the next morning, all four of them were on their way back to Paris.

EPILOGUE

Shenanigans

Remi and Julien's parents didn't speak to them for nearly three months. It wasn't so much that Remi and Julien had extorted million of dollars from them. The families admitted they'd been greedy and in the wrong. But Remi and Julien had waited until the day after the press conference to tell their parents the truth—their wedding in Paris hadn't been legally binding.

Remi was never quite sure what Merrick had said to the French minister or how much he'd bribed him to perform the wedding and sign off on a semi-official-looking document. She didn't know and she didn't want to know. The ruse of the wedding had been for her sake anyway. Merrick knew Remi would never be able to lie to her parents with a straight face and say she'd gotten married if she hadn't actually gotten married. She knew they weren't *legally* married, but it was enough that she could look her mother in the eyes and say she and Julien had had a wedding. It was a dirty trick to convince their parents that they had no choice but to give up the rivalry now that the only Montgomery daughter had married the only Brite son. If the two families had merged, the two businesses were merged whether they liked it or not. Remi and Julien considered this little hoax of theirs nothing more than justice served for the high-priced and dangerous fraud their parents had been perpetuating.

With their parents still not speaking to them, Remi and Julien spent Christmas Day alone together. But the privacy suited them just fine as Julien asked her to marry him on Christmas Eve. They celebrated her "yes, yes, absolutely yes" by making love under the tree. Twice.

By New Year's, their families jointly forgave them at a dinner party Remi hosted to announce the engagement. Remi wanted to believe this forgiveness was born of their parents seeing the error of their ways, repenting and turning over a new leaf. In truth, she knew it was the reams of good press that Capital Hills and Arden Farms had gotten all over the world that had changed their minds. The "moving, touching, awe-inspiring" decision to bury the hatchet and create a charity that would let sick, disabled and needy teens and tweens spend time riding and caring for horses would cement the Brites' and the Montgomerys' legacy of giving and service to Kentucky and the horse-racing world. Every racing family in the tristate area had stepped up and pledged money to the cause. The Raileys had already written them a check for five million that their parents accepted in an embarrassingly staged photo op at Verona Downs.

Remi didn't take it too personally that her parents and Julien's parents were taking all the credit for the idea of the charity and acting as if this merger had been their plan all along. All Remi cared about was Julien, her horses, Merrick and Salena, and their plans for the future.

And getting her fiancé into bed.

In November, they'd moved into their new place—the

farm her parents had, against their will, given them for the nonprofit. By January it already felt like home. Julien had started school again at the University of Kentucky and was working toward a degree in psychology so he could better help the kids who would be served by their charity. At age twenty-six, she was officially engaged to a college freshman and no one could stand in the way of her love for Julien anymore. Remi had set up an office for him in the rambling Colonial farmhouse that had come with the acreage. He looked so cute sitting at his desk, hunched over his textbook and laptop, that all she could do was stroll in and stand there waiting for him to notice her.

The wait lasted about one second.

"Oh damn," Julien said, sitting back in his chair. He stared at her wide-eyed.

"I told you I still had the outfit." She'd put on her old dressage clothes for him—tan jodhpurs, leather gloves, velvet coat, white shirt with tie and, of course, the riding boots.

"I can't breathe," Julien said.

"Should I call Dr. Salena?" Remi batted her eyelashes. "Or should I just take the outfit off?"

"Option B, please." Julien got out of his chair and came to her. He cupped the back of her neck and kissed her with bruising force.

She pulled away and grabbed him by the hand. They'd had office sex shortly after moving in. Some things were better left to a big, comfortable bed.

Once in their bedroom, Remi shut and locked the door behind her. Merrick had been hanging out at the house earlier, and she didn't want him wandering into their bedroom by accident. Knowing him, it wouldn't be an accident. She pushed Julien down onto his back and straddled his hips.

He put up no fight whatsoever.

"I love the braid." Julien said, tugging on the end of her French braid.

"Easiest hairstyle to fit under a helmet," she said as she unbuttoned his shirt. She ran her gloved hands all over his bare chest.

"Plus I can do this," he said, gently tugging on her braid to pull her head back. He rose up and kissed the exposed flesh of her neck.

"Even better." She purred the words as she kissed him again, long and deep and with all the love and passion she felt for him. And she did love him and knew she would love him forever. The stars would burn out long before her love for him did.

Once more she pushed him onto his back. She unzipped his jeans and wrapped her gloved hand around him.

"That is weird," he said, gasping slightly.

"Never had leather on your cock before?"

He shook his head.

"Never. I kind of like it though. Maybe." He narrowed his eyes. "No, wait. I definitely like it. No, I love it."

She rubbed him gently, feeling him getting harder and harder with every long stroke. Julien propped up on his elbows and watched her touch him. Well…if he wanted a good show, she could give him a good show.

Remi sat back and lowered her head, taking him into her mouth.

Julien collapsed onto his back with a groan.

"Oh my God…" he breathed. "Blow job with you in riding clothes…Teenaged Julien is somewhere in the past with a massive hard-on and a smile on his face and he has no idea why."

Remi didn't answer. Her mouth was a bit too busy to speak at the moment. She ravished him with her tongue, licking him from base to tip and back down again. She tasted the first drops of his semen. Good. She wanted him to come in her mouth. He'd been working so hard today. He deserved it.

She gripped the base and worked her mouth up and down his length. At first she went slowly to tease him. Once his breathing hastened, she moved faster to coax him to the edge. She loved hearing him pant for her, loved seeing his eyes closed and his lips parted and his fingers digging into the sheets of the bed they shared and made love in nearly every night. She hoped that somewhere out there their parents were quietly fuming that she and Julien had won. Life was undeniably good right now and was only getting better.

In a few months, life would get even better than it was right now, and she couldn't wait to tell him why.

Julien's breathing quickened as she sucked him deep into her mouth. He said her name once and then came with a rush, his shoulders coming off the bed from the reflex of pleasure.

She swallowed every drop of him and wiped off her lips with the back of her gloved hand.

"You are the sexiest woman alive," Julien breathed. "It's ridiculous. If you got any sexier, I don't think I'd make it."

"No?" she asked, as she got off the bed and unzipped her boots. "What if I did this?"

She slipped out of her jodhpurs.

"The world becomes a better place when you take your pants off," Julien said, watching her every move.

"What if I did this?" She slipped her feet back into her boots and zipped them again.

"You without pants on and wearing boots is..." Julien paused.

"What?"

"Well, it could only get better if—"

Remi slithered out of her panties and tossed them onto Julien's chest.

"That," he said.

She straddled his hips again and rubbed herself gently against him.

"I'm going," he sighed. "I'm not going to make it. You're so sexy it's killing me…I'm going…going…"

On the "gone" he grabbed her and flipped her onto her back. In a tangle of arms and legs and laughing, Remi ended up with her head hanging off the bed and Julien between her thighs. Good place for him to be, the perfect place even.

With quick, rough fingers, Julien unbuttoned her coat and the white shirt underneath. He kissed her breasts as he gently teased her clitoris. When he'd grown hard again, he pushed deep into her.

And because she knew he would be disappointed if she didn't, Remi crossed her legs at the ankles and rested the heels of her riding boots on his lower back.

"Even better," he whispered.

"Even better what?" she asked.

"Your boots on my back during sex is even better than I dreamed it would be."

"It really is," she agreed. "This was a good idea."

"The best idea. I think this is the new best day of my life."

"It's about to get better," Remi said.

"How?"

"Because we've got a baby on the way."

Julien froze midthrust.

"A baby?" He stared at her, his eyes huge with shock. "But…they said I couldn't have kids. And I'm still in school. And we aren't actually married. And we haven't talked about…but still, that's—"

"Not me, silly," she said. "I'm not the one pregnant."

"Not you? Then who?" Julien looked so wildly relieved she almost laughed at him.

Remi patted the side of his face and grinned. "Shenanigans."

★ ★ ★ ★ ★